Boulevard Comedy Theatre in Germany

Boulevard Comedy Theatre in Germany

by

Daniel Meyer-Dinkgräfe

Cambridge Scholars Press

Boulevard Comedy Theatre in Germany
by Daniel Meyer-Dinkgrafe

This book first published 2005 by

Cambridge Scholars Press

15 Angerton Gardens, Newcastle, NE5 2JA, UK

British Library Cataloguing in Publication Data
A catalogue record for this book is available from the British Library

Copyright © Cambridge Scholars Press

All rights for this book reserved. No part of this book may be reproduced, stored in a retrieval system, or transmitted, in any form or by any means, electronic, mechanical, photocopying, recording or otherwise, without the prior permission of the copyright owner.

ISBN 1-904303-48-X

Contents

Introduction..3

Chapter One:
The Boulevard Comedy Theatres in Germany..............................12
    Ambience...12
    Artistic Managers..18
        Ingrid Braut and Alfons Höckmann,
        Komödie Düsseldorf.. 19
        Dieter Rummel, Die Komödie TAP, Darmstadt........ 23
        René Heinersdorff, Theater an der Kö, Düsseldorf.... 23
        Gerd Schlesselmann, Komödie Dresden................. 23
        Carl Philip von Maldeghem, Komödie im
        Marquardt, Stuttgart.. 24
        Roland Heitz, Komödie Kassel............................. 24
        Ronald F. Stürzebecher, Theater in Cronenberg,
        Wuppertal..25
        Angelika Ober, Boulevard Münster 25
        Florian Battermann, Komödie am Altstadtmarkt,
        Brauschweig...26
    Organizational Structures and Artistic Policies................... 27
        Organizational Aspects....................................... 27
        Management Sharing.. 28
        Productions per Year...30
        Casting Policy: National Stars
        Versus Local Actors.. 30
        Touring... 33
        Seats and Prices.. 34

Chapter Two:
The Repertory of Boulevard Comedy Theatres in Germany............... 36
    The Set...40
    Telephone Conversations...44
    Efficient Scene Endings.. 45
    Professional Clichés... 47
    The Generation Gap.. 52

    Couples as Central Characters..56
    Elements of Farce...63

Chapter Three:
Aspects of Translation...73
    Cultural Contexts..73
    Language...76

Chapter Four:
Production and Reception of Boulevard Comedy..........................80
    Acting in Boulevard Comedy...80
    Directing Boulevard Comedy..83
    Media Coverage..87
    Audiences...88

Chapter Five:
Future Research Potential..90

Bibliography..95

Appendix A: Cities with Boulevard Comedy Theatres....................99

Appendix B: Plays..102

Index..106

ACKNOWLEDGEMENTS

Several of the details I provide in this book are based on conversations with the theatre artists and research in the archives of the various theatres. I wish to extend my gratitude to the artistic managers, actors, directors, dramaturges and personal assistants for the time to talk to me. I am grateful for research grants from the University of Wales Aberystwyth Research Fund and to the British Academy, which enabled me to travel to Germany on three occasions to carry out this research. Finally, my thanks to my department for granting me research leave to write the book.

INTRODUCTION

Twenty major German cities have a total of twenty-four theatres specializing, at a high level of sophistication, in presenting light comedy. Theatre artists, journalists, academics and critics refer to them as *boulevard comedy theatres* that present productions of *boulevard comedy*. According to official annual statistics of sold seats, in almost all cases, boulevard comedy theatres have been able to attract larger audiences than municipal or state theatres in the same cities. Such commercial success is remarkable in a fiercely competitive market. Boulevard comedy theatres are predominantly privately run, with only two exceptions that receive public subsidy. They have their own typical ambience and principles of artistic management and casting. There are playwrights, actors, directors and designers who work almost exclusively in boulevard comedy, developing highly specialised approaches to their work. The plays are light comedy, sometimes with darker undertones, often placing their ordinary middle class characters within extraordinary situations, much in the tradition of farce.

Geographically, twenty-three of the twenty-four boulevard comedy theatres in Germany are spread evenly across the former West Germany: Berlin, Bochum, Bonn, Braunschweig, Cologne, Darmstadt, Düsseldorf, Duisburg, Frankfurt, Fürth, Hamburg, Hannover, Heilbronn, Karlsruhe, Kassel, Münster, Munich, Stuttgart and Wuppertal. Dresden is so far the only city of the former East Germany to possess a boulevard comedy theatre. Seventeen boulevard comedy theatres have the word *comedy* in their name, spelt either conventionally Komödie, or more progressively, Comödie. Some theatres refer to their location in their name, either the city (e.g., Komödie Düsseldorf[1]), or an area or within the city: for example, Düsseldorf's second boulevard comedy theatre is located near the main shopping street of the town, Königsallee, or Kö for short and calls itself Theater an der Kö. The boulevard comedy theatre in Cologne is located close to the famous cathedral and thus calls itself Theater am Dom. The only boulevard comedy theatre to be located within a five-star hotel is Munich's Komödie im Bayerischen Hof. One of the three boulevard comedy theatres in Wuppertal is called m&m theater, taking the first letters of the founder and artistic directors' last names: Misiorny and Mueller. Another boulevard comedy theatre named after its founder is the Waldau Theater Komödie Bremen, which started as a theatre dedicated to presenting plays in the regional dialect of Bremen and added boulevard comedy to the repertory and the word Komödie to its name only in 2002.²

At the head of each boulevard comedy theatres in Germany is the *Intendant*, who combines artistic and managerial - administrative functions. The restricted budget of boulevard comedy theatres does not often allow a split of artistic and managerial functions, such as is more and more frequent at larger German municipal or state theatres. Across the country, the older artistic managers, who founded the major boulevard comedy theatres in the 1950s and 1960s, are gradually retiring and making way for a new generation with fresh ideas and initiatives for their theatres. The majority of boulevard comedy theatres have to survive without subsidies of any kind, though some receive a minor subsidy. One of the boulevard comedy theatres that is most heavily subsidised, the Komödie im Marquardt in Stuttgart, still relies on box office receipts for forty per cent of its annual budget. The Komödienhaus in Heilbronn is the exception in the boulevard comedy theatre scene in Germany, in that it is a newly built venue of that town's fully subsidised municipal theatre.

The twenty-four boulevard comedy theatres in Germany together produce more than 100 plays per year. They are a considerable factor in Germany's theatre scene. Yet academic consideration of boulevard comedy theatre in Germany has been very limited. In his 1968 history of comedy, Prang explicitly excludes the discussion of boulevard comedy because such plays do not really want to do more than entertain their audiences for one night in the theatre (1968: 364). Similarly, Schoell, writing particularly about post-second-world-war French drama, states that the sole intention of boulevard theatre is to entertain its audiences. The spectators are those who want to spend a good amount of money to purchase pleasant entertainment without much strain and if the boulevard theatres do not offer such entertainment any more, such spectators are likely to go to a striptease club instead (Schoell, 1970: 69). The plays in the boulevard theatres, Schoell argues further, have been the same since they first appeared: they did not undergo any genuine development of either language or form. Haida disagrees: a development has taken place when boulevard comedies deny their spectators the happy ending, characteristic of conventional plays in the boulevard comedy canon (1973: 157). Weckherlin summarises that in Germany, boulevard comedy theatre carries the stigma of the trivial, with its synonyms of banality, shallowness, flatness, meaninglessness and insignificance (2001: 21). Leisentritt's 1979 Ph.D. thesis, *Das Eindimensionale Theater*, shares this general approach. Weckherlin's 1992 MA thesis discusses the production of Ayckbourn's *Henceforward* at one of the two Berlin boulevard comedy theatres directed by the renowned Peter Zadek (b. 1926), focusing on the four ways in which this production broke the norms of theatre in general and boulevard comedy theatre in particular: first, the fact that Zadek, the artistic manager of the largest state theatre (Deutsches Schauspielhaus Hamburg) directed at a privately run boulevard comedy theatre; second, what Zadek made of the production itself; third, that actors usually appearing at the state theatres now made their debuts at boulevard comedy theatres; and finally, the impact such a production has on the audience of a boulevard comedy theatre.

Boulevard comedy theatre is unique to Germany: only in Germany are there twenty-four of these theatres across the country, with up to three per city. There is nothing comparable in the United Kingdom, the United States of America or in France, where the term *boulevard comedy* originated. Regional theatres in the United Kingdom have comedies in their repertories, as does the Royal National Theatre (RNT) in London, including the plays that feature in the repertories of the boulevard comedy theatres in Germany. Occasionally, successful productions from regional theatres or the RNT transfer to the West End of London; rarely are comedies mounted directly for West End venues. Between 1925 and 1933, Tom Walls (1883-1949) produced thirteen farces at the Aldwych Theatre in London, which became known collectively as *Aldwych Farces*. Ben Travers (1886-1980) wrote nine of those. Between 1950 and 1966, Brian Rix (b. 1924) produced farces at the Whitehall Theatre in London, which became collectively known as *Whitehall Farces* (Smith, 1989). It was here that Ray Cooney (b.1932) learnt his trade as an actor and writer of farce. In 1983, Cooney founded the Theatre of Comedy company, for which he bought and refurbished the Shaftesbury Theatre in London (Chambers, 2002: 174). The company still exists today, but has long since its foundation broadened its spectrum of productions beyond comedy. Thus there are today no theatres in the United Kingdom that specialise exclusively in comedy.

In the United States of America, Dinner Theatre is a phenomenon that originated in 1959 in Washington. D.C. Lynk defines it as 'the combination of a quality meal and a live theatrical presentation, presumably in the same room, at a value-oriented ticket price.' (1993: 1) The venues vary in size, seating between 125 to 1130. Some cities have dinner theatre multiplexes, with more than one stage. Food is available from a self-service buffet, or the venues provide table service. As far as the repertory is concerned, most dinner theatres present musicals, such as *Singin' in the Rain*, *The King and I*, *South Pacific*, or *Oklahoma*. Sometimes producers spend up to $100,000 on lavish sets and costumes that compare well with productions of the same musicals on Broadway (Lynk, 1993: 37). Occasionally, dinner theatres put on non-musical, straight plays, with comedy dominating. Here, the comedies by Neil Simon (b. 1927) are favourites, because 'they involve small casts, are easy to produce, can be star vehicles and are box office draws.' (Lynk, 1993: 38) Managers of dinner theatres face a double challenge in having to deal efficiently with both the artistic and the culinary sides of their business. In summary, the American phenomenon of dinner theatre is not the same as boulevard comedy theatre in Germany.

The term and the concept of boulevard comedy theatre originated in France and indeed the continuing boulevard comedy theatre scene in this country is most closely related to that in Germany. Paris still has a number of theatres that continue the tradition, such as the Le Théâtre Edouard VII, La Comédie de Paris, Théâtre des Variété and La Comédie des Champs-Élysées. It is, therefore, important to understand the origins of the genre in France and its developments to the present day, to establish whether Germany took over and today merely continues a tradition begun in France, or whether (and where) boulevard comedy theatre in Germany went its own ways that make it different from developments in France (Corvin, 1989, and Brunet, 2004).

The term *boulevard* originally means *fortification*, referring to the fortifications of Paris built by the knights Templars. In the late seventeenth century a section of that fortification was torn down on the northeastern outskirts of Paris and in its place a promenade was built, initially known as *Promenade des Remparts*. This promenade attracted 'cafés, sideshows and other entertainments and became a sort of all-year-round fair.' (McCormick, 1982: 12) It became especially attractive to Parisians during those months of the year when the two seasonal fairs, Saint-Germain and Saint Laurent, were closed. In 1778, the promenade was paved, which made it even more attractive. It became known, due to the origins, as the *boulevard du Temple*.

Carlo Goldoni (1707-93) provides the following description of the boulevard du Temple, which is worth quoting in full because it serves well to give a vivid impression:

> An infinite crowd of people, an amazing quantity of carriages, street merchants darting in and out amongst … the horses with all sorts of merchandise, chairs set upon the sidewalks for those who want to watch—and for those who want to be watched--, cafés fitted up with marionettes, acrobats … giants, dwarfs. Ferocious beasts, sea monsters, wax figures, automatons, ventriloquists, [and] the surprising and enjoyable sideshow of the wise physicist and mathematician Comus. (Root-Bernstein, 1984: 42)

In the boulevard theatres, the French guard was on duty, maintaining order and pushing audiences tightly on to the benches. In this way the largest boulevard theatres would seat around 400.

Three theatres enjoyed royal protection under Louis XIII (1601-43) and Louis XIV (1638-1715), the Opéra, the Comédie Française and the Comédie Italienne. They had, by law, the privilege to perform the major genres of theatre, as well as, for the Opéra, music, dance, ballet and opera. Despite those theatres' protest against competition, the authorities tolerated minor theatrical entertainment on seasonal fairgrounds and on the boulevard du Temple. The political divide relating to privileges went hand in hand with an aesthetic division: the three privileged theatres were to present high art to an educated elite, while the boulevard venues were to cater for a less well educated audience predominantly with low comedy and farce (Root-Bernstein, 1984: 22).

Over time, these establishments began to call themselves theatres. They did so to the dismay of the three major companies, whose superior position was maintained not only through royal patronage, but also through a clear distinction as to where the three bill-posters employed in Paris had to stick up placards announcing theatre productions in selected places across the city: placards for the three major companies were placed very distinctly and separately from those for the 'minor theatres'. The major competing newspapers in Paris at the time, *Journal de Paris* and *Petites Affiches*, printed daily listings of theatre programs, initially only those of the major three companies, from the early 1780s also those of the minor theatres, but clearly set apart in the page layout. Censorship helped to reduce the quality of plays offered on the boulevard, because from 1769 the official censors asked two actors from the royally supported theatres to censor the submissions from the boulevard theatres (McCormick, 1982: 12). Boulevard theatres were not permitted to use either plays from the repertory of the Comédie Française, or adaptations and parodies of classical farce, or even existing characters from plays in the Comédie Française's repertory. The detractors of boulevard theatre regarded what they had left to them as 'bawdy, gross, trivial, empty, an unwholesome mix of obscene and detestable plays …[with] the most cringing buffooneries.' (Root-Bernstein, 1984: 27)

What kind of plays did these people come to see? Predominantly farce and comedy, with stock characters like old men, lovers, peasants, artisans and tradesmen, as well as masked characters that had their origins in Italian *commedia dell'arte*. The plots were urban, predominantly set in Paris and initially showed a middle- or lower- class world—a predominance dictated by censorship. Only with the decline of censorship did more high middle-class and upper class characters enter the plays—reflecting an increasing percentage of upper class spectators. The plot was typically that of a love intrigue—a young man meets a young woman, they fall in love, but the parents threaten their union. Servants help the young lovers and against all odds they get married in the end. Comedies constructed around this formulaic love intrigue were dominant not only at boulevard theatres, but also at the royal theatres. While at the royal theatres, the number of such formulaic comedies declined after 1750, the formula was maintained conservatively at the boulevard theatres until 1794. From 1780 onwards, at boulevard theatres side plots were added, which emphasised themes such as 'social equality, nature and sentimental love.' (Root-Bernstein, 1984: 99) With the decline of the formulaic love intrigue as the basis of plots in the major theatres from 1750 onwards came the rise of bourgeois drama, characterised by a notable a shift of the plot's focus from love intrigue towards sentimental love ties. The royal actors in their roles as censors, however, barred such bourgeois drama from boulevard theatre. Boulevard plays initially parodied the new sentimental trends of the royal theatres, later adopted them successfully, changing plot elements typical of the love intrigue formula to suit the new mode. The parent's consent, an essential element of the love intrigue formula, is not achieved through the servants outwitting their masters: rather, the disapproving parents are sentimentally convinced that the initially rejected lover of their son or daughter will be an acceptable, even desirable marriage partner for their offspring after all. Numerous plays for boulevard theatre of the later eighteenth century did away altogether with the love intrigue formula, emphasizing sentimental encounters between people that went beyond the limited themes of love intrigue.

In 1784, law was changed so that boulevard theatres now had no longer to obtain a license to perform from the police, but permission, against payment, from the Opéra, a move to assist that royal company get out of debt. Two entrepreneurs bought one of the boulevard theatres, the Variètés-Amusantes, in the process dispossessing its previous owners and directors. They relocated the theatre into a newly built venue and openly declared their intention on making this theatre into the second best in France, to rival the Comédie Française. In 1786, plays at the Variètés-Amusantes were exempted from censorship, although some of the enforced differences of the repertory remained. Censorship by two royal actors was discontinued in 1789 and in 1791 the privileges of the royal theatres were abolished. As a result, the number of theatres in Paris rose from nine to seventy. The plays in the repertory of boulevard theatres developed towards melodrama and sensational plays, leading to the boulevard du Temple being dubbed 'boulevard du Crime.'³ By 1830, the middle classes had taken over political, economic and cultural power. Increasing industrialization meant an increase in the contrast between city and countryside, with the city becoming more and more important. Paris became interesting both for people living in Paris and for the people from the provinces, as France's cultural centre. For members of the rising middle classes, visiting the capital was an event that culminated in attending the theatre; the locals, too, saw the theatre as an expression or a characteristic of city life.

Wehinger has analysed the state of boulevard theatre around the year 1857; her methodology is historical, placing developments in theatre repertory in a meticulously researched historical context (1988). Among the aspects she discusses in depth as influential, together, for the development of boulevard theatre is first the influence exerted by the various political regimes that characterised nineteenth century France, with all its hopes and disillusionment. Secondly, the renewal of the boulevards prior to the world exposition of 1867 is significant: the authorities closed down all the minor venues in favour of a selected and refurbished few. Finally, the relation between boulevard theatres and boulevard press is important: in several cases, the same authors wrote both the plays and the articles. Wehinger points out that in revues, which the boulevard theatres presented regularly at the end of the year and which provided a kind of retrospective of the past year's events, boulevard theatre itself featured prominently: they offered comical insights into backstage life, intrigues, conflicts, and dealt, in addition, with the audiences of those theatres. The revues put on stage personifications of the major state theatres: for example, the Opéra appeared as a Chinese person on horseback, speaking a language incomprehensible to the boulevard theatre audiences (Wehinger, 1988: 69). In addition, the revues included pointed references to major successes of the boulevard theatres' season; because all items on the revue's agenda had to be short and direct, the plots of those successful shows left out any secondary lines of plot development, reducing the plot to a key issue, such as the father-son relationship for plays by Alexandre Dumas (1802-70).

In 1862 the original boulevard du Temple gave way to the Place de la République and the term boulevard theatre changed to refer to the 'commercial, non-subsidised theatres in Paris that offer entertainment to the affluent bourgeoisie.' (Stanton and Banham, 1996: 40) Here, comedy and especially farce developed as the major fare. Eugène Scribe (1791-1861) developed his techniques of the well-made play across his comedy vaudevilles and historical-political comedies, such as *Le verre d'eau* (The Glass of Water) (Arvin, 1924). Victorien Sardou (1831-1908) developed those techniques further (Shaw, 1911: xxii-xxvii), and Eugène Labiche (1815-88) used the formulae of the well-made play in his farces.

Critics consider the plays of Georges Feydeau (1862-1921) as the pinnacle of the development of farce from their Greek origins in Aristophanes, via stages of Rome (Plautus), medieval farce in France, Shakespeare's *The Comedy of Errors*, 'afterpieces' in France and England of the seventeenth century and full-length farces in the eighteenth and early nineteenth centuries, up to Scribe, Sardou and Labiche (Drechsler, 1988: 13-22). In particular, Feydeau's farce is closest to tragedy, as Aldous Huxley suggested: 'Tragedy is the farce that involves our sympathies; farce, the tragedy that happens to outsiders.' (1951: 43)[4]

Tristan Bernard (1866-1947), Paul Géraldy (1885-1983), Jacques Deval (1890-1972), Marcel Achard (1899-1974), André Roussin (1911-1987), Pierre Barilley (b. 1923) and Jean-Pierre Grédy (b. 1920) continued this line, as do Félicien Marceau (b. 1913), Françoise Sagan (b. 1935) and Françoise Dorin (b. 1928). It is important to note that in France, plays popular in boulevard theatre did not only comprise the farces and comedies by the authors listed above. André Antoine's reforms of French theatre, followed by those of Copeau, brought vibrant contemporary plays on the stage: they were also subsumed under the heading of boulevard theatre, as compared with and opposed to, the classics. After the Second World War, other more serious plays, by authors such as Anouilh and Sartre, were added to the repertory. Since the 1960s, however, the number of boulevard theatres in Paris has been reduced due to an increase of the subsidised sector. Remaining theatres began to import comedies from the United Kingdom and the United States of America and some even managed to secure subsidies themselves. Among the current generation of authors writing for the boulevard comedy theatres of Paris are Yasmina Reza (b. 1959) and Eric Emmanuel Schmitt (b.1960).[5]

Boulevard theatre in Germany builds on the developments of comedy in general, of farce in the United Kingdom, of the plays popular in American dinner theatre and on the tradition of boulevard theatre in France as far as the repertory is concerned. Chapter two will deal with issues of repertory in detail. Boulevard comedy theatres in Germany came into existence after the Second World War and have grown in popularity ever since. There is nothing comparable in France, the United Kingdom and the United States of America to the wide distribution of boulevard comedy theatres in Germany. In that sense the phenomenon of boulevard comedy theatres is a phenomenon that is unique to Germany. This book provides a description and an analysis of boulevard comedy theatre in Germany. An analysis of boulevard comedy theatres in Germany with respect to ambience, artistic managers, artistic policies and artistic structures forms the first chapter. The second chapter discusses major characteristics of the plays presented on the stages of German boulevard comedy theatres. Special reference is given to German dramatist Curth Flatow's plays in comparison with other authors of boulevard comedy theatre in the repertory. The third chapter deals with aspects of translation and the cultural transfer of comedy and laughter. The forth chapter focuses on aspects of production and reception, dealing in turn with actors, directors, media coverage and audiences. The book concludes with a range of suggestions for further research.

Two appendices complement the main body of the book: appendix one lists the boulevard comedy theatres in Germany, providing details about artistic directors, seating capacities, ticket prices and websites. Appendix two provides a list of plays referred to in this book with writer, original title of the play and its translation into English.

Notes

1 The name of that theatre from its foundation in 1968 until 2004, when, a year after the theatre was taken over by a new management, it was renamed Komödie Düsseldorf an der Steinstrasse.

2 It ceased to be a boulevard theatre in 2004, though, after the city state of Bremen discontinued its subsidy. For that reason I do not count this theatre among the twenty-four boulevard comedy theatres in Germany.

3 For a detailed history of the boulevard entertainment in eighteenth century Paris, see Robert M. Isherwood, *Farce and Fantasy: Popular Entertainment in Eighteenth Century Paris*. New York: Oxford University Press, 1986. For the development in the 19th century, see Harold Hobson, *French Theater Since 1830*. London: John Calder, 1978.

4 Paul Macroux discusses the serious aspects of Feydeau's farce in 'Georges Feydeau and the 'serious' farce', *Farce*. Themes in Drama, Volume 10. edited by James Redmond. Cambridge: Cambridge University Press, 1988, 131-143. Volker Klotz discusses Feydeau's farce in the context of his history of bourgeois theatre of laughter in *Bürgerliches Lachtheatre: Komödie, Posse, Schwank, Operette*. Reinbek bei Hamburg: Rowohlt, 1987.

5 See Chapter 4 in David Bradby and Annie Sparks, *Mise end Scène: French Theater Now*. London: Methuen Drama, 1998, 118-126, for a discussion of the current private theatre scene in Paris, the star actor system and the work of Schmitt and Reza in particular.

CHAPTER ONE

THE BOULEVARD COMEDY THEATRES IN
GERMANY

Ambience

What are the boulevard comedy theatres buildings in Germany like and what do artistic managers do to create a specific boulevard comedy theatre ambience? The Komödie Düsseldorf, the Theater and Komödie am Kurfürstendamm, Berlin and the Boulevard Münster serve as representative examples. Ingrid Braut and Alfons Höckmann founded the Komödie Düsseldorf in 1968 in the centre of that city. They remained as artistic managers until 2003, when Helmuth Fuschl and Paul Haizmann took over. Braut and Höckmann created a distinctive brand for their boulevard comedy theatre. On approaching the theatre building, one immediately saw the name, Komödie, in characteristic large red-orange letters, above the entrance. The same text appeared on the cover of all souvenir programs sold to accompany each production mounted at the Komödie. The entrance, under the flat protruding roof that carries the marquee, has glass showcases on the right, with portrait photos of the cast and stills from the production currently showing. As the visitor enters, the box office is on the same level; next to it is a door leading to the café associated with the Komödie. The way to the foyer leads down a flight of stairs, with posters from previous productions on the walls and an announcement for the next production in large letters, sometimes accompanied by photos above eye level facing the visitor who descends the staircase, or waits at the box office. The foyer, downstairs, is a wide, round space, with, to the right of the staircase, restrooms, the wardrobe, which serves as a bar during the interval, an emergency staircase, two entrances to the auditorium and a wall space that is used as a large bulletin board with photos of the stars who have appeared at the Komödie in the past, most of them with personal dedication and autograph. The colour scheme matches that at the entrance, with various shades of red and orange. Formally dressed usherettes sell programs at the entrances to the auditorium, also checking audience tickets as they enter. Thus the building is intimate and straightforward. Photos of the cast give the spectators a feeling of familiarity and there is a characteristic colour scheme that audiences have come to associate with Komödie. Formally dressed usherettes lead to a feeling of the audience being important and respected.

The two boulevard comedy theatres in Berlin, almost adjacent to each other on Berlin's major 'boulevard', the Kurfürstendamm, are the oldest boulevard comedy theatres in Germany. The Kurfürstendamm-Theater opened in 1922 with a production of Curt Goetz's *Ingeborg*, with Goetz himself (1888-1960) and Adele Sandrock (1863-1937) in the cast. In 1924, Max Reinhardt (1873-1943) asked the architect Oskar Kaufmann (1873-1956) to build the Komödie in the mode of a castle theatre; the opening production was Goldoni's *Il servitore di due padroni* (Servant of Two Masters). In 1927, dramatist Ferdinand Bruckner took over the Kurfürstendamm-Theater, which was renamed Theater am Kurfürstendamm, followed in 1928 by Reinhardt, who asked the same architect who had built the theatre, Kaufmann, for major refurbishments. In 1932, Reinhardt withdrew from the Theater am Kurfürstendamm and for the 1932/1933 season there were altogether six artistic directors in a row. In 1933, finally, Hans Wölffer (1904-76) took over both the Komödie and the Theater am Kurfürstendamm. In 1942, under the Nazi regime, the two theatres were nationalised; they burned down in 1943 when an allied plane was shot down and crashed nearby. The Komödie reopened in 1946, the Theater am Kurfürstendamm in 1947. The Komödie was taken over by Dr Kurt Raeck (1903-1981) in 1949, where Hans Wölffer joined him in 1950. Wölffer had the theatre refurbished and redesigned and continued as sole artistic director. In 1962, he also took over the Theater am Kurfürstendamm, which had been the home of the Freie Volksbühne from 1949 to 1962. Hans Wölffer's two sons, Jürgen and Christian, trained as actors and gained experience as actors and directors at theatres across Germany. In 1965 they joined the management of the two Berlin boulevard comedy theatres, which they took over after their father's death in 1976. Jürgen Wölffer's son Martin, who chooses to spell his name Woelffer, is the third generation of the Wölffer family involved in the artistic management of the theatres. He took over the general artistic management from his father and uncle in 2004. Both theatres have been refurbished several times since the 1960s and the Wölffers opened newly built boulevard comedy theatres in Hamburg--the Komödie Winterhuder Fährhaus (established 1988) -- and Dresden, Komödie Dresden (established 1996) (http://www.theater-am-kurfuerstendamm.de/).

In Münster, founding artistic manager of the Boulevard Münster, Angelika Ober, was successful in getting a leading architect, Dieter Sieger to design the new boulevard comedy theatre for this city (Ober, 2003). Here is how Sieger described that design on his website, closer to the time of the Boulevard Münster's opening—the site has since changed and omits the text below:

> Dieter Sieger has built a new theatre in the heart of his hometown of Münster. Inspired by all the theatres of the world and by one in particular – the Teatro La Fenice, (...) Dieter Sieger has – in conjunction with his team leader Benedikt Sauerland – created an ambience full of elegance and love of detail. In an area of 350 square meters 121 guests can be seated in the Boulevard Münster on chairs specially designed by Dieter Sieger. Framed by stylised facades made of Spanish sandstone, which looks like the region's own Baumberger Sandstein, the interior design reflects the roots of light theatre – the place where stories, romances and tales of human relationships are performed.
>
> The lobby quotes elements that are typical of theatre. The entrance, for instance, looks like a large glass curtain framed by the facade. The door greets the guest with forty-two gold-plated handles reflecting the individual reception given to each guest who – irrespective of how tall they are – will find their own personal handle to open up the doors to the world of theatre. A friend of Dieter Sieger, François Gervais, who lives in Amsterdam, was contacted to create an unmistakable logo in his own style. Once the visitors have left the everyday world behind them, they float along a lavish deep-red carpet towards the stairs. These lead the visitors downwards around a sculpture that rises through the stairwell from the basement. The visitors then enter the auditorium over a ramp-like bridge where a surprisingly generous view opens up to them.
>
> The dominating colour of red interacting with the golden surfaces conveys an air of elegance and formality. The entire theatre is blanketed by a sky of stars, a sophisticated drama of light, offering a fascinating prelude to the show. The members of the audience taking their places in the seats with engraved numbers get the impression that the performance is given individually for each one of them. The view to the stage is focused through a gold-plated strictly geometric frame quote. The funny plays are presented like the individual elements of a style a baroque artist would use on deep-black Oregon pine wood. The adjacent bar invites guests to a drink before the performance starts or to a glass of champagne during the break. Dark mahogany and black Nero Marquina marble have been used here to remind visitors of English smoking salons or old industrial clubs.
>
> One particular gem are the toilets on the top floor. As a major designer of objects used on the sanitation sector, Dieter Sieger was particularly concerned to create a room that reflects the flair of the world. The design of the wash places represents a miniature theatre. A stage made of Nero Marquina marble houses the archetype of a basin, a sink turned from white Statuario marble.

The tap – a design by Dieter Sieger for Dornbracht – is like a well-spring attached to the wall. Special designs by the stainless steel manufacturer Kuhfuss even give the towels a radiant staging. The room's design is rounded off by a floor laid out in the classical chessboard design of white marble and black Nero Assuluto granite.

In less than three months, a team of more than forty tradesmen created a highlight of interior design over an area of more than 350 square meters. More than 250 square meters of Danish textiles were used for the 121 armchairs. More than 250 lamps were fitted to the ceiling and almost five kilometres of cable installed to control the stage engineering and air-conditioning system (which only uses fresh air) (http://www.boulevard-muenster.de/). Altogether, Sieger's design has not only enriched the theatre life of Münster, but has also demonstrated that unusual projects built to a standard of perfection are still possible in Germany.

The boulevard comedy theatres in Germany appeal to their audiences through these distinct features of architecture, relating to the entrance area, a café-restaurant associated with the boulevard comedy theatre, public areas outside the auditorium and the auditorium itself. What happens inside the auditorium before the performance begins and as the curtain rises, also follows set conventions, which audiences take for granted and expect to see fulfilled. The auditorium of the Komödie Düsseldorf seats 376 spectators in comfortable red plush folding seats. The stage is fifteen meters wide and five meters in depth. The red stage curtain, which opens to both sides, is nine and a half meters wide. The curtain is usually drawn when the audience enters and there is soft, unobtrusive background music. The start of performances at the Komödie Düsseldorf is also characteristic for boulevard comedy theatres in Germany: when the lights go down, the general background music changes to the music specifically chosen for the production and increases in volume. Many theatre productions in the world will feature music before the curtain opens and it is likely that music increases in volume when the lights go dark. However, there are as many productions whose directors decide not to have either pre-show music or music when the lights go down. So while the use of music in boulevard comedy theatre is not unique as such, it is still a characteristic that distinguishes it from other forms of theatre. The same goes for the curtain, which is opened quickly where technically possible and the set on stage is revealed only once the curtain is open. As the express purpose of boulevard comedy theatre is to please its audiences in as many ways as possible, the set is conventionally beautiful to look at regarding shapes and colours. It often draws the first round of applause from the audience.

Audiences in Germany usually do not applaud when the performance starts, so again this audience response is characteristic of boulevard comedy theatre. In the case of Komödie Düsseldorf under the Braut – Höckmann management, since leading Düsseldorf-based fashion designer Hanns Friedrichs created most of the costumes anew for the major characters in most productions, when leading female characters entered the stage, another round of applause welcomed them in recognition of the style and beauty of their costumes. It is not customary for audiences in Germany's municipal or state theatres to respond to the first appearance of an actor on stage with applause; hence, the applause for the costumes at Komödie Düsseldorf was specific to this particular boulevard comedy theatre in Germany.

In addition to features of architecture and conventions in the auditorium just before and at the beginning of the performance, which are typical for boulevard comedy theatres in Germany, artistic managers place an emphasis on an easily identifiable layout and design of advertising flyers, brochures and particularly program booklets, which every spectator will buy before the performance and keep as a souvenir. Over the thirty-five-year history of the Komödie Düsseldorf under the Braut-Höckmann management, the basic program layout and format changed only once. Initially, programs were an approximate A5 portrait in shape, each with a different colour for the front and back cover, with the familiar design of the word 'Komödie' in bold black letters at the top, followed, underneath, by the details 'Boulevard-Theater Düsseldorf Ingrid Braut / Alfons Höckmann' and underneath that the address and phone details of the theatre's administration. At the centre of the page, again in bold letters differing from production to production in style and font appeared the title of the play. At the bottom of the page, the same for each production, appeared details for ordering tickets. From the mid-1990s, the format changed to a square. Front and back covers were white, with a thick orange block in the upper half of the front cover, showing the season in bold black and the production within that season in larger bold white to the left (96 5 97 would signify the 5th production of the 1996/97 season) and the familiar Komödie 'Boulevard-Theater Düsseldorf Ingrid Braut / Alfons Höckmann' to the right. At the bottom of the page was the title of the play, in bold orange, underlined and under the line the name of the dramatist, with a hint of the genre, for example: Komödie von und mit Gunter Philipp (comedy by and starring Gunter Philipp). In addition to the new size and the new layout of information included in the previous format, the new format also included a photo of the main actor and/or director.[1] The new artistic directors, Fuschl and Haizmann, went back to the A5 portrait format, kept the font and style of the word Komödie (capital K in orange, the rest of the word lower case bold black, flushed right), kept the orange and black print on white background for the front cover, with the title and writer details towards the top of the page only a little underneath the Komödie heading, kept a photo, but not necessarily of performers or writer, all so as to maintain tradition, but cut the sub-title Boulevard-Theater Düsseldorf, replacing it with the more sober Düsseldorf GmbH and, a season after taking over, changing it to 'Komödie Düsseldorf an der Steinstrasse.' (http://www.komoedie-duesseldorf.com/index.htm).

Apart from the change in cover and shape, the contents of the programs at the Komödie Düsseldorf hardly changed at all under the artistic management of Braut and Höckmann. With different sequences for each program, the recurrent features were photos of the play's writer, accompanied by a brief biographical note, a brief note on the topic / contents of the play, portraits of the actors appearing in the play, as well as of the director, set designer and costume designer, in many cases also accompanied by biographical details. There were usually three pages of credits, listing the German title of the play, with the original language title in brackets below, if applicable and the writer(s) of the translation if applicable. The first page listed the production team, i.e., director, set designer, costume designer, assistant director(s), lighting designer, make-up artist and hairstylist and stage management. That page also credited the set builders, the production photographer and the performance rights. The following two-page spread listed the character names against the names of the performers. The remainder of the program was taken up by short articles (hardly more than one page each) of entertaining material relating to the topic covered in the play, or to boulevard comedy in general. Headings included, for example: Why are so few comedies written in Germany? Can theatre change its audiences? What are we laughing about? Or: The most important person of the theatre. Finally, each program had a listing of credits for the articles in it, an invitation to take out a subscription and an announcement of the next production, or the entire next season, with the title, writer, major cast, director and designers of set and costume. Many pages of the program carried advertising.[2] A typical program ran from between twenty-four to thirty pages (forty pages for the thirty-year special edition).

At Boulevard Münster, season brochures and production programs share the unique logo of that theatre, as well as the characteristic colour scheme of red and black on glossy white paper. Programs carry the credits on the third page, together with information about the next production, contact details and website. The following pages provide information about the contents and photos of and information about the dramatist, the actors, the designer and the director as well as information about the contents and credits of the next production. Those pages also carry rehearsal photos of the productions. Pages with such information are interspersed with pages dedicated to advertisements.[3] Aspects of architecture and conventions of performance and program notes are thus the major factors apart from the productions themselves that distinguish the boulevard comedy theatres in Germany from German municipal or state theatres.

Artistic managers

Who runs the boulevard comedy theatres in Germany? It is no exaggeration to state that all boulevard comedy theatres in Germany are closely linked to their artistic directors, who in many cases identify their lives with their theatre. The Wölffer family (Berlin, Hamburg, Dresden), the Durek / Heinersdorff families (Cologne, one of the two Düsseldorf boulevard comedy theatres and, until 2003, one of the two Munich boulevard comedy theatres) and the long-serving artistic directors in Hannover, Darmstadt and Frankfurt, among others, are cases in point. In comparison, for the vast majority of state, municipal and regional theatres, an artistic director/manager who stays for more than five years with one theatre is an exception. The stage biographies of Ingrid Braut (1926-2001) and Alfons Höckmann (b. 1923), who founded the Komödie Düsseldorf in 1968, serve as an example for the fully trained actors with long-established careers in state of municipal theatres in Germany, who, at some stage in their careers, decided to found a boulevard comedy theatre. In the same category are the members of the Wölffer family in Berlin, Katinka Hoffmann and Horst Johanning at the Contra Kreis Theater in Bonn, Inge Durek and Barbara Heinersdorff at the Theater am Dom, Cologne (and, until 2003, the Kleine Komödie am Max II in Munich), Claus Helmer at the Komödie Frankfurt and James von Berlepsch at the Neues Theater, Hannover.

Dieter Rummel is an example for a theatre artist manager who has spent all his adult life in boulevard comedy theatre, the Komödie TAP Darmstadt. He occupies a category of his own, as does René Heinersdorff, who is currently the only independent artistic manager of a boulevard comedy theatre who comes from a family of artistic managers of boulevard comedy theatres, which provided his inspiration to found his own, the Theater an der Kö in Düsseldorf. Gerd Schlesselmann's stage biography represents the artistic managers recruited by the artistic management of the Berlin boulevard comedy theatres to run their Dresden and Hamburg branches. Jürgen Mai, who succeeded Schlesselmann in Dresden in 2003, Rolf Mares, who ran the Komödie Winterhuder Fährhaus in Hamburg from 1988 to 1999 and Michael Lang, who has been in charge since 1999, are in the same category.

Carl Philip von Maldeghem and Roland Heitz took over the artistic management of existing boulevard comedy theatres, the Komödie im Marquardt, Stuttgart and the Komödie Kassel, respectively. Margit Bönisch did the same at the Komödie im Bayerischen Hof, Munich, in 1992 and Michael Derda at the Waldau Theater Komödie Bremen in 1994; Heidi Vogel-Reinsch took over at the Kammertheatre in Karlsruhe following her founder-husband's death in 1998. Braut and Höckmann passed on their artistic management of the Komödie Düsseldorf to Fuschl and Haizmann in 2003. Ronald F Stürzebecher founded his own boulevard comedy theatre, Theater in Cronenberg, Wuppertal, after having gained experience as a dramaturge with Wuppertal's municipal theatre. Angelika Ober successfully made the transition from a long-serving actress with the municipal theatre in Münster to founding her own boulevard comedy theatre, Boulevard Münster. In a comparable way, actors and directors Jochen Schroeder and Rolf Berg joined forces to establish the Komödie Bochum Veranstaltungs GmbH. Florian Battermann, finally, is the youngest artistic director of a boulevard comedy theatre in Germany—he founded the Komödie am Altstadtmarkt in Braunschweig in 2003 at the age of thirty. These biographical surveys thus represent the full range of artistic managers of boulevard comedy theatres in Germany.

Ingrid Braut and Alfons Höckmann, Komödie Düsseldorf

Ingrid Braut was born in 1926 in Hamburg.[4] Her father was a merchant, her mother a secretary. From her father she inherited her desire to remain independent; her mother played the piano (her grandfather was a piano maker with Steinway&Sons) and Braut learned playing at the age of five. Early on she developed the desire to become an actress, taking up acting and singing lessons as well as ballet classes while still at school. The arts were also represented on her father's side of the family: one uncle was film-star Hans-Hermann Schaufuß. Frigga Braut, one of her father's sisters, was a star at the old Kammerspiele in Hamburg and later a notable character actress at the Schauspielhaus in Düsseldorf. It was Frigga Braut, along with Ernst Leidesdorff, the artistic director of the Thalia Theater in Hamburg, who trained Ingrid Braut for the theatre. Frigga was a strong influence on Ingrid, who felt close to her, even if life under her tutelage was not always easy. Thus, Ingrid Braut remembers that on one occasion, Frigga woke her up in the middle of the night asking her to immediately recite Gretchen's prayer from Goethe's *Faust*, to see how well prepared she was.

Ingrid Braut obtained her first professional employment at the age of seventeen, in 1943 in Vienna. She appeared as Paula in *Der Raub der Sabinerinnen* (The Abduction of the Sabien Women), which starred Schaufuß. For the last years of the war, Braut provided entertainment for wounded soldiers in field hospitals. Alfons Höckmann was born in 1923, the fifth of eleven children, in Dortmund. His father owned a bakery. Höckmann, like his future wife Braut, never wanted to pursue a different career than that of an actor. He took acting classes and in 1941, while still attending Gymnasium he was successful in his second attempt to gain admission to what was then leading drama school in Germany, the Westfälische Schauspielschule in Bochum. Its director, Saladin Schmitt accepted him as the last student before the school had to close, later in 1941, because of the war. Höckmann soon became a member of the theatre company in Bochum, which was led by Schmitt. He was recruited and spent the years of 1943-45 with the navy in Tuscany.

After the war, Höckmann returned to the company in Bochum. When the theatre reopened, in 1945, with a production of Grillparzer's *Weh dem der lügt* (Liars, Watch Out), Höckmann met his future wife, Braut, whom Schmitt had asked to join his company from Hamburg. The costumes for the production were made from blankets, the bombed-out theatre did not have a back wall and the audience had to bring coal for heating. Nevertheless, the company's enthusiasm was unbroken, fuelled by newfound freedom. Braut appeared in *Die Ratten* (The Rats) by Gerhart Hauptmann, *Dr.med. Hiob Prätorius* by Curt Goetz, Noel Coward's *Private Lives* and *Charley's Aunt* by Brandon Thomas. Höckmann appeared in Molière's *Tartuffe*, Shakespeare's *Hamlet* and also in *Charley's Aunt*.

Soon, Braut and Höckmann moved on to his employment with the company in Baden-Baden, where he first played the title role in Schiller's *Don Carlos*, at the age of twenty-two. They were married and Braut continued her singing lessons. The journey from employment to employment went on: first they moved, after half a year, to Munich, where for the next three years they gained valuable experience in the classical repertory at the Junges Theater. To finance the furniture for their flat, they founded a singing duo called *Die Evergreens*, performing a range of popular songs of the time, mainly on the radio. Following the currency reform, the Junges Theater had to close down; they moved to the Schaubude, performing cabaret. After Munich, they went to Lübeck, where Höckmann found roles as romantic hero, playing parts in Sartre's *Les Mains Sales* (Dirty Hands), Schiller's *Fiesko* and *Wilhelm Tell*, Eugene O'Neill's *Mourning Becomes Electra*, Wilde's *Salome* and Shakespeare's *Taming of the Shrew*. Braut became a soubrette in music theatre, singing parts in *Frau Luna*, *Der letzte Walzer* (The Last Waltz), *Opernball* and, at the age of only twenty-five, she was among the youngest singers to appear as Frau Fluth in *Die lustigen Weiber von Windsor* (The Merry Wives of Windsor). In those days Braut and Höckmann met several fellow-actors whom they would later invite to work with them at the Komödie Düsseldorf, for example Peter Oehme.

In 1951, Höckmann joined the company in Nuremberg. He appeared with Doris Schade in Grillparzer's *Des Meeres und der Liebe Wellen* (The Waves of the Ocean and of Love), Ernst Barlach's *Der Graf von Ratzeburg* (The Count of Ratzeburg) and in Jean Anouilh's *Colombe* and Shakespeare's *Twelfth Night*. In Nuremberg and in neighbouring Regensburg, Braut sang various important roles in opera and operetta, such as the Queen of Night in Mozart's *Zauberflöte* and the leading roles in Verdi's *Rigoletto* and *La Traviata*. In 1952, the couple's daughter Andrea was born, who later joined her parents as an actress at the Komödie Düsseldorf.

In 1954, Höckmann and Braut moved to Zurich, where Höckmann joined the theatre under the artistic directorship of Oskar Wälterlin. Important members of the company included Will Quadflieg, Werner Hinz, Johanna Moissi, Therese Giehse, Gustav Knuth and Heidemarie Hatheyer. Höckmann was employed as youthful hero of the classical repertory, but he also appeared in plays by Anouilh, Sartre and O'Neill. At the age of thirty-three, he played his second Don Carlos, appeared in the first German production of Faulkner's *Requiem for a Nun*, in Anouilh's *Leocadia*, in Herman Wouk's *The Caine Mutiny Court Martial* and in Tolstoy's *Licht scheinet in der Finsternis* (A Light Shines in the Darkness). German novelist Thomas Mann saw a performance of *Leocadia* and wrote in his diary: 'To the theatre in the evening. Leocadia by Anouilh. Some of the actors amused me, a certain Alfons Höckmann, something of a provincial Romeo, played the prince.' Most important for Höckmann during his years in Zurich was working with director Leopold Lindtberg, who impressed him with his enormous skills (Höckmann, 2001). Sometimes Lindtberg had to mount big productions, such as Shakespeare's *Henry IV*, within a rehearsal period of three weeks. While based in Zurich, Höckmann also appeared as a guest actor in Bern and Lucern—in the latter he was given the opportunity for his first work as a director, for the operetta *Gräfin Mariza*.

When Höckmann moved to Zurich, Braut initially joined him, but there was no work for her there. So she commuted, whenever she was free, between Zurich and the Landestheater in Salzburg, where she was employed as leading soprano for opera and operetta. Her debut was with Johannes Heesters (b.1903) in *Hochzeitsnacht im Paradies* (Wedding Night in Paradise), later to be followed by the role of the doll in *Hoffmanns Erzählungen* (The Tales of Hoffmann), Musetta in *La Bohème* and Sapphi in *Der Zigeunerbaron*. After Salzburg, Braut worked in Bern and Vienna. A special highlight was the European tour of *Das Land des Lächelns* (The Country of Smiles) with celebrated tenor Helge Roswaenge.

In 1959, Höckmann and Braut were sacked because Höckmann sided with the director in a political dispute, but Karl-Heinz Stroux, artistic director of the Schauspielhaus in Düsseldorf, almost immediately invited Höckmann to join his company, taking over the position vacated by Siegfried Wischnewski (1922-1989). Besides his work as a stage actor, Höckmann increasingly appeared on television. Braut sang at the opera house in Rheydt, where she was surprised to find in Horst Heinze a director working at a level comparable with internationally renowned theatres.[5] At the beginning of the 1960s, Höckmann and Braut finally settled down, after some seventeen moves of household. While Höckmann was busy at the Schauspielhaus in Düsseldorf and on radio and television, Braut appeared at various theatres in the area: the Theater am Worringer Platz, the Theater an der Berliner Allee in Düsseldorf and the Theater am Dom in Cologne. This is how she gradually returned from singing to speaking parts and was introduced to boulevard comedy. She also taught phonetics to chorus leaders at the conservatory in Düsseldorf for four years.

In 1968, the Steinstrasse theatre building in Düsseldorf was available; Höckmann had become less satisfied with his work at the Schauspielhaus and Braut, too, was ready for independence. They founded the Komödie-Boulevardtheater Düsseldorf, with Peter Thomas as dramaturge (he later became artistic director of the Kammerspiele in Düsseldorf) and Horst Heinze as major director apart from Höckmann himself. Heinze's wife, Annemarie, initially took on the financial management of the new company. Ulrich Jacob, the Komödie's long-serving senior set designer, was heavily involved in refurbishing the theatre and getting it ready for the opening night on 20 August 1968. The first production was André Roussin's *Die Lokomotive*, starring Lil Dagover.

Dieter Rummel, Die Komödie TAP, Darmstadt

One of the founding fathers of boulevard comedy theatre in Germany is Dieter Rummel (b. 1939). He took acting lessons during his apprenticeship as a forwarding merchant and founded Die Komödie TAP (Theater am Platanenhain) in 1960, at the age of twenty-one. Since then he has selected and directed most of the three to four productions per year and has also played many leading parts in them. His personal devotion to his theatre is particularly evident in that he recovered from a major stroke (in 1989), which would have brought other careers to a complete end; he regained nearly full mobility from complete right side paralysis that had him wheel-chair bound for several months and regained full control of his speech. Today, if spectators do not know about his disability, they will not notice it in performance (Rummel, 2003).

René Heinersdorff, Theater an der Kö, Düsseldorf

René Heinersdorff, member of the artistic management of the Theater am Dom, Cologne and until 2003 of the Kleines Theater am Max II in Munich and sole artistic manager of the Theater an der Kö in Düsseldorf, was born in 1963 and thus belongs to the younger generation of boulevard comedy theatre artistic directors. After his Abitur, he studied German and Philosophy at the University in Düsseldorf and received his training as an actor and director from Harald Leipnitz (1926-2000), a respected film and television actor who, later in his career, turned increasingly to acting in and directing boulevard comedy. Heinersdorff also took singing lessons with Ruth Grünhagen, a renowned Düsseldorf-based teacher. He appeared at theatres in Berlin, Hamburg, Munich, Cologne, Düsseldorf, where he directed more than forty productions. In addition he was very active on television, not only in parts in individual episodes, but also in ongoing parts for long-running series and as a director (http://www.theatreanderkoe.de/).

Gerd Schlesselmann, Komödie Dresden

The founding artistic manager of the Komödie Dresden was Gerd Schlesselmann, in office from 1996 to 2003. He worked there under the overall management of the Wölffer family in Berlin. He was born in 1942 in Hamburg; from 1972 to 1979 he was artistic manager (*Künstlerischer*

Betriebsdirektor) at the Deutsches Schauspielhaus in Hamburg under artistic director Ivan Nagel and in the same position for the 1979/80 season at the Schauspielhaus Bochum with artistic director Claus Peymann. From 1980 to 1985 he served as deputy artistic director at the Deutsches Schauspielhaus in Hamburg; in that city he also developed the alternative arts venue Kulturfabrik Kampnagel. During those years he started his collaboration with Peter Brook, whose German tour of *The Man Who* he organised in 1993. From 1985 to 89 he managed the Stella Musicaltheater, which brought *Cats* to the Operettenhaus in Hamburg, *Starlight Express* to Bochum and *Phantom of the Opera* to Hamburg. From 1989 to 1991 Schlesselmann returned to the Deutsches Schauspielhaus in Hamburg as artistic leader under the artistic director Michael Bogdanov and took on the role of interim artistic director for a time. Before joining the Komödie Dresden, he served as artistic director of the Hamburger Kammerspiele for a season (Schlesselmann, 2001).

Carl Philip von Maldeghem, Komödie im Marquardt, Stuttgart

In 2002, Carl Philip von Maldeghem took over the artistic management of the Komödie im Marquardt, Stuttgart from his predecessor Elert Bode, who had been in office since 1976. Born in 1969, von Maldeghem studied law and philosophy, taking a Ph.D. in the philosophy of law. Later he studied acting and directing at the Lee Strasberg Institute in New York. He worked as assistant director at the American Repertory Theatre in Cambridge (United States of America) and on Broadway; he was press officer and personal assistant to Gerard Mortiers at the Salzburg Festival and served as an assistant to Peter Stein. From 1997 onwards he was director and personal assistant to the artistic director at the Karlsruhe state theatre (http://www.schauspielhaus-komoedie.de/geschichte/index.html). On the occasion of taking over the Komödie im Marquardt, von Maldeghem promised to maintain the tradition Bode established, while introducing the audiences to new actors and directors (von Maldeghem, 2002: 147-9).

Roland Heitz, Komödie Kassel

Roland Heitz took over the artistic management of Komödie Kassel in 2001, which had been founded in 1950. His most immediate predecessors were Horst Lateika, in office from 1987 to 2000 and Gerhard Fehn, who served for only the 2000/2001 season. Heitz trained at the Hochschule für

Kunst und Theater in Saarbrücken (1976-79) and worked as an actor in Regensburg, Krefeld / Mönchengladbach, Hannover, Zurich and Hamburg. In Hamburg he added directing to his credits. At the beginning of the 1990s Heitz was artistic leader and manager at the Altonaer Theater in Hamburg. From 1995 - 98 he was deputy artistic manager at the Stadttheater Herford. In addition, he directed freelance in Münster, Bremen, Detmold, Erfurt, Wien, at the dome festival in Gandersheim and at the Torturmtheater Sommerhausen, which is led by Veit Relin (http://www.komoediekassel.de/intro.html). Heitz's term of office ends with the 2004/5 season.

Ronald F. Stürzebecher, Theater in Cronenberg, Wuppertal, founded 1986

The artistic manager of Theater in Cronenberg, Wuppertal, abbreviated TiC, Ronald F. Stürzebecher, was initially the dramaturge of the Wuppertal municipal theatre. He had established a group of young performers at the theatre who wanted to experiment with their art. When the city had space available in a former, by then long-disused school, they asked Stürzebecher to put on a production there. He did and from there continued, eventually becoming independent and focusing increasingly on boulevard comedy (Stürzebecher, 2003).

Angelika Ober, Boulevard Münster

Angelika Ober founded Boulevard Münster in 1997. Before that, Ober had been a member of the company of the municipal theatre in Münster for thirteen years. That theatre's artistic director had resigned and the theatre's management suggested to Ober to seek employment elsewhere. The reason: were she to continue in employment, she would soon have reached the threshold of reaching tenure and the theatre's management did not wish to confront an incoming artistic director with members of the company he/she would not be able to sack if he/she did not like them. Ober could have joined other companies in Germany. However, she had come to like Münster, had her partner and friends there and decided to become independent. While still with the municipal theatre in Münster, she had already begun to feel uneasy with some of the practices characteristic of municipal theatres in general: for example, finding out the casting of new productions from the notice board and realizing which of the colleagues, who get all the great parts, spent their holidays with the relevant directors. Thus, when Ober was advised to resign, she did so, but stayed on in Münster. She sat together, literally, with her sister Elke, her partner Peter Pittermann and her mother and made plans for her own theatre. She bought a computer, took courses in business administration, read plays, put together a first season, talked to actors and directors she knew and approached Franz-Josef Görtz, the owner of the space which was later to become the Boulevard Münster, at that stage still a discothèque, but not very successful as such. Görtz initially declined, but two months later came back to Ober and asked whether she was still interested. At that stage she had been looking at a different venue, where she would have had to shoulder all the costs. She met with Görtz and presented him with her by now well-developed ideas for the first season, including a breakdown of costs. They agreed that having the available space re-designed and built as a theatre, together with the necessary equipment, would cost one million DM. Görtz agreed to pay three quarters of it. Ober's bank agreed to provide her with a loan needed to obtain the rest of the funds on the basis of Görtz's involvement. Ober serves not only as manager and artistic director: she regularly performs in the plays in her theatre's repertory and directs at least one production per season. Her sister Elke and her partner Peter Pittermann share the design work (Ober, 2003).

Florian Battermann, Komödie am Altstadtmarkt, Brauschweig

The artistic manager of the Komödie am Altstadtmarkt in Braunschweig is Florian Battermann (b. 1973). His theatre, which he founded in 2003, is the most recent addition to the boulevard comedy theatre scene in Germany. The theatre is truly a family business: his wife runs the box office. Battermann's mother and mother-in-law run the business office, his father-in-law designs and builds the sets and his brother is in charge of contracts and personnel. Battermann began writing plays at the age of six and has so far written five boulevard comedies. He studied German and history, initially also theology. He took acting lessons and obtained his first employment as assistant director and actor with the boulevard comedy theatre in Hannover, Neues Theater. James von Berlepsch, its artistic manager, became Battermann's mentor. In 1998 Battermann directed his own first play, *Weekend mit Winnetou* (Weekend with Winnetou) at the Neues Theater; it was revived in 1999 at the Komödie Kassel and followed by the world premiere of his play *Drei plus eins gleich Halleluja* (Three plus One Equals Halleluja) at the Komödie Nuremberg in 2000. From 2000 until the opening of the Komödie am

Altstadtmarkt, Battermann was also deputy artistic manager at the Kleines Theater in Bad Godesberg (http://www.komoedie-am-altstadtmarkt.de/).

Organizational Structures and Artistic Policies

The artistic managers of German boulevard comedy theatres have developed distinct artistic and commercial policies in running their theatres efficiently. Since most boulevard comedy theatres in Germany are unsubsidised, the challenge their artistic managers face is to balance commercial needs and artistic ideals. Artistic and commercial policies discussed in this section relate to the occasional cooperation with other boulevard comedy theatres and the decision to open up branches in other cities with an idea at transferring productions from one venue to others to save production costs. Policies also include decisions as to seating prices, the number of productions per year and casting either local actors or national film and television stars. Policies relating to the repertory and the nature of additional, one-off performances are covered in a separate chapter.

Organizational Aspects

Organizationally, boulevard comedy theatres in Germany range from a shoestring set-up to a structure comparable to a small municipal theatre. Sabine Misiorny and Tom Müller's m&m Theater, founded in Wuppertal in 1993, is a two person company. Their productions are all written in-house: Müller writes the broad outline and dialogue and Misiorny provides the details. They also co-direct. For reasons of marketing and publicity, they have chosen to use a pseudonym for writing and directing: T. B. Thompson, an homage to the British tradition of comedy writing and indeed reviews sometimes comment on the 'British' bite' or sense of black comedy in T. B. Thompson's plays and the 'British' edge of his productions. Dictated by financial necessity, the plays by Misiorny and Müller never require more than two performers (who at times play multiple characters, though) and can be put on with minimal requirements to set, costume and lighting design (Misiorny and Müller, 2003).

The TAP Komödie Darmstadt is a representative of the small organization without subsidies. Artistic manager Dieter Rummel also serves as actor and director, his wife Monika runs the box office and the company's finances and Volker Seibel is in charge of the design and technical aspects (Rummel, 2003).

At the other end of the spectrum is the Waldau Theater Komödie Bremen. Up to the end of 2003, the theatre was predominantly subsidised by the federal city state of Bremen, allowing the theatre to employ up to thirty administrative staff in positions comparable to established and fully subsidised municipal or state theatres. One member of staff deals with publicity and marketing, there are two administrators, three dramaturges, a graphic designer, two set designers, five stage technicians, one sound engineer, three lighting operators, two carpenters, two staff each in charge of props, costume, make-up and general technical maintenance and three box office staff.[6]

The Theater in Cronenberg (TiC), Wuppertal, aims at professional standards although it employs both trained actors who did not pursue a full-time career in the profession, but want to act in their spare time and young hopefuls who seek the experience TiC may offer them to prepare for drama school, or, in exceptional circumstances, to lead to professional employment without drama school. Anyone who wants to act may approach the theatre's management and undergo several interview stages and castings; those considered promising, from among both the trained and the untrained actors, will get a chance. Rehearsal periods are usually eight weeks with rehearsals on weekday evenings and all day weekends. Especially for people who are in full employment over the week, this means a serious commitment. If actors fail in their commitment, they are given one opportunity to explain themselves and improve, but contracts are such that they may be dismissed at very short notice if they do not improve (Stürzebecher, 2003).

Management Sharing

The two Berlin boulevard comedy theatres share their central management with the Berlin branches, the Komödie Winterhuder Fährhaus in Hamburg and the Komödie Dresden; the artistic policies of Berlin and Hamburg are equally closely coordinated: productions are regularly scheduled to transfer from one venue to the other (http://www.theatre-am-kurfuerstendamm.de/), while Dresden is artistically more independent due to the differences in audiences, which make easy transfers impossible. For its first two seasons, from 1996 to 1998, the Komödie Dresden presented mainly comedies originally produced in Berlin, with casts including actors from the Dresden area in minor parts, but mainly with stars that the Berlin boulevard comedy theatres found to attract Berlin audiences. Slowly, but definitely, Dresden's artistic manager Schlesselmann realised that both the kinds of plays and the stars imported from Berlin did not have similar magnet function as they had in Berlin. The Komödie Dresden did not sell enough seats and its survival was at risk. While it was part of the German Democratic Republic, Dresden had been cut off from West German television reception due to its geographical location and thus her inhabitants did not know many of the television stars imported from West Germany's Berlin. Even solo one-off performances by eminent actors, such as Christian Quadflieg, would end up with only 200 spectators in the theatre that seats 664. Schlesselmann managed to convince the Wölffers that a complete rethink was needed. Over the next seasons he developed Dresden's own repertory, abandoning plays by Alan Ayckbourn (b.1939), which had been particularly unsuccessful at the box office[7], and stars from the former West Germany. Instead, Schlesselmann's decision to include in the repertory Curt Goetz, 1950s and 1960s French comedies, such as Claude Magnier's *Oscar* and stage versions of famous films, such as *Arsenic and Old Lace*, *Harold and Maude* and *Die Feuerzangenbowle* (Burnt Punch) and even a classic, Molière's *Le Malade Imaginaire* (The Hypochondriac) proved successful. Schlesselmann characterises his choice of repertory as comparatively conservative. The casts are almost exclusively made up of actors who were trained and had worked in the former German Democratic Republic; they had come to prominence either in the municipal theatres or through television, in many cases both. Schlesselmann added a studio stage to the main theatre, for readings and smaller-scale visiting productions, which are often one-person shows presented by popular actors well known and thus attractive to the audience (Schlesselmann, 2001).

There are other boulevard comedy theatres in Germany that share the same managements. The Comödie Bochum Veranstaltungs GmbH, led by Patricia Frey, Rolf Berg and Jochen Schroeder, runs the boulevard comedy theatres in Bochum, Duisburg and Wuppertal and, from 2001 to 2002, also one in Dortmund. Productions regularly transfer between those three venues, with Berg and Schroeder also directing and acting (http://www.comoedie-bochum.de/). Transfers of productions were equally part of the Heinersdorff's policy at their boulevard comedy theatres in Düsseldorf and Munich, as is occasional cooperation with the boulevard comedy theatres owned by the Comödie Bochum Veranstaltungs GmbH (http://www.theater-am-dom.de/ and http://www.theaveranderkoe.de/).

In Stuttgart and Frankfurt, a variation of management sharing is in place: here the artistic managers are not only in charge of the boulevard comedy theatres in these cities, the Komödie im Marquardt and the Komödie Frankfurt, respectively: von Maldeghem in Stuttgart also runs the Altes Schauspielhaus and Claus Helmer in Frankfurt took over the artistic management of the near-bankrupt Fritz Rémond Theater im Zoo, leading it out of the red within one year (Helmer, 2003). The audiences of the two Frankurt theatres that Helmer manages are distinct and the season of six plays at the Fritz Rémond Theater im Zoo contains a mixture of classics, such as Lessings *Nathan der Weise* (Nathan the Sage) and plays that feature in conventional boulevard comedy theatre repertories, such as Kesselring's *Arsenic and Old Lace* (http://www.diekomoedie.de/). In Stuttgart, too, the repertories and audiences of the two theatres run by von Maldeghem are different from each other (http://www.schauspielhaus-komoedie.de/).

Productions per Year

Following its foundation season with eight productions, the Komödie Düsseldorf operated on the basis of six productions per year, which would each run for about two months.[8] Höckmann and Braut reduced that number to five (each running for just under two and a half months) from the 1973/74 season, but when the second boulevard comedy theatre, Theater an der Kö, opened in Düsseldorf in 1994, the number had to be raised again to five for the theatre to remain financially viable in view of the competition (Höckmann, 2001). When Fuschl and Haizmann took over the Komödie Düsseldorf in 2003, they raised that number even higher, to seven per season, leading to a reduced run for every production of less than two months (http://www.komoedie-duesseldorf.com/index.htm). At the Komödie Kassel the season consists of eight productions (http://www.komoediekassel.de/). Misiorny and Müller's m&m Theater in Wuppertal has staged one production per year, which they presented at a variety of venues in the Wuppertal area. In 2003 they began collaboration with the Theater in Cronenberg (TiC), also in Wuppertal, using one of TiC's spaces for their productions, charging the same ticket prices as the TiC and co-directing a TiC production in autumn 2003 (Misiorny and Müller, 2003).

Casting Policy: National Stars Versus Local Actors

The mainstream productions at the two boulevard comedy theatres in Berlin feature major stars as audience magnets. Throughout the 1970s and well into the 1980s, such stars had been keen to appear at the Berlin boulevard comedy theatres, because the money they were paid was better than for both film and television and at other theatres in Berlin. Times have changed, however, in at least two ways. The first reason is aesthetic: it can become difficult to find all-star casts for two productions running parallel, because there are not that many stars left from film who are keen to play boulevard comedy. According to Martin Woelffer, television stars are not as attractive to the audiences: 'they are on the screen in the spectators' homes every evening anyway, so spectators are not as desperate to see these stars live on stage.' (2001) The second reason is financial: the salary the Wölffers can offer is no longer competitive. They pay their actors per performance, with a salaries budget for a single performance of between €2,000 and €3,000, with a tendency towards the lower of those two figures. The average pay for an actor is thus €150 per performance, with €200 or €250 counting as really good pay. Stars get more, by negotiation, but the Berlin boulevard theatres still cannot compete with a salary of €1,000 per performance at one of the larger Berlin municipal or state theatres (Woelffer, 2001). Despite these aesthetic and financial obstacles, the Wölffers have been successful in attracting actors like Gisela Mai, Daniel Morgenrot, Michael Mertens, Michael von Au and Klaus Maria Brandauer as actors and Peter Zadek as director. In 2001, film actress Katja Riemann played the female lead in Ayckbourn's *Intimate Exchanges*. Martin Woelffer doubts whether Riemann would have agreed to play in a plain farce (Woelffer, 2001). She was attracted, he assumes, by the dark undertones critics and academics frequently associate with Ayckbourn's plays.[9] Woelffer hopes that this model continues to work in future and that once film stars have thus been led to overcome their reluctance of appearing on the stage of a boulevard comedy theatre, it might be possible to persuade them to appear in more traditional plays of the repertory (2001).

Actor Ralf Komorr und financial manager Fritz Hendel share the artistic management of the Kleine Komödie am Max II in Munich, after taking over from the Heinersdorff management (http://www.kleinekomoediemuenchen. de/). The new Munich management faces the challenge shared with other younger generations in charge of a boulevard comedy theatre, such as Komödie Düsseldorf and in part the Wölffer stages in Berlin, Dresden and Hamburg, of keeping the older generation of spectators happy by continuing the kind of repertory they are accustomed to, while on the other hand attempting to attract new audiences with plays new to the boulevard comedy theatre repertory. Thus, in the 2003/4 season they chose Daniel Karasek, a director associated with well received productions at municipal and state theatres, to direct Ayckbourn's *Time of my Life*. The female lead was cast with Gudrun Landgrebe, an actress well-known to audiences from serious parts on film and television, who ventured into boulevard comedy for the first time here (Komorr, 2003).

Most attractive to the audience and most rewarding for the plays in which they appear, are actors who have made their name in boulevard comedy, such as Wolfgang Spier and Herbert Herrmann. At the age of 84, Spier is the leading actor, director and translator in the genre. Artistic managers and the press like call him the uncrowned king of boulevard comedy theatre in Germany and Spier has referred to Herrmann as his natural heir (Spier 2001, 2003).

In contrast to Berlin, Boulevard Münster has done without star actors famous from film and television (Ober, 2003). In Stuttgart, artistic manager Bode did not favour a star system, a policy his successor, von Maldeghem, has continued (http://www.schauspielhaus-komoedie.de/). To be able to compete with the other theatres in Stuttgart, both the municipal and the independent ones, the seasons have to be planned two years in advance. As Bode's wife put it: 'the Altes Schauspielhaus and the Komödie im Marquardt have to clearly find and define their profile.' (2001) Neither of the two theatres has constant companies: both work with guest actors employed play by play. Thus long-term planning is in the interest of actors and directors as well. The Komödie im Marquardt does not use stars well-known from film and television. The reason for this is not only financial, but also related to Bode's attempts not to undermine his theatre's local impact. Thus, although many of the actors are employed on the guest contract basis, they come again and again and have developed into genuine local stars (2001). This local aspect of boulevard comedy theatre in Germany is at least equally important at the Komödie Dresden, where stars from the former West Germany do not attract audiences.

While some boulevard comedy theatres, such as those in Berlin and Munich depend on stars from film and to a lesser extent television as audience magnets and others have been able to establish their positions without national or international stars, the Komödienhaus in Heilbronn is in a special position. The municipal theatre in Heilbronn has a main stage, a smaller stage and a new venue, the Komödienhaus. The actors appearing in the Komödienhaus are part of the municipal theatre's company. The theatre's artistic managers use the Komödienhaus to present predominantly comedy, but not the kind that dominates the repertory of the other twenty-three boulevard comedy theatres in Germany, but more demanding, satirical and critical material. In the 2003/4 season, the Komödienhaus presented six new productions: *Hysterikon*, written by Ingrid Lausund who works as dramatist in residence and director at the Deutsches Schauspielhaus in Hamburg, is set in a supermarket and takes a satirical take on capitalist consumer culture in Euro-times. Ayckbourn's *Season's Greetings*, which opened on 22 November 2003, in time for Christmas, was characterised in the website announcement as an amusing farce of society written by a master of situation comedy. Ayckbourn is here advertised and marketed as light comedy, rather than emphasizing the darker undertones of his plays. Frank Wittenbrink's revue *Sekretärinnen* (Secretaries), featuring eight secretaries who talk and sing about their open and hidden thoughts and desires, has been immensely successful in numerous different productions across Germany. The Komödienhaus Heilbronn did not mount its own production, but invited that of the Theater Wechselbad , Dresden, directed by Gerd Schlesselmann, who was founding artistic manager of the Komödie Dresden from 1996 to 2003. The world premiere of Penny Black's *Making Babies* deals with Jake, a young medical student. He has abducted fertility expert Professor Jackson to take revenge because Jackson 'created' him for his grandparents as a surrogate for his deceased father. Sabine Habeke's *der himmel ist weiss* (the sky is white) shows one woman in her relationship with three men, across various stages of her life. The play combines precision in its depiction of ordinary and extraordinary situations with a delicate sense of humour. Neil LaBute's *The Shape of Things* is a contemporary, sophisticated, humorous but dark version of the Pygmalion motif—student Adam is transformed by his contact with Evelyn, an extraordinary art student (http://www.theater-heilbronn.de/).

Touring

The artistic managers of two boulevard comedy theatres, Margit Bönisch at the Komödie im Bayerischen Hof in Munich and Braut and Höckmann at the Komödie Düsseldorf, founded touring companies in addition to their permanent theatres. They sell productions either from the repertory of their permanent theatres, or productions specially produced for touring purposes, to smaller theatre venues that do not maintain their own companies.

Seats and Prices

On average, each of the twenty-four boulevard comedy theatres in Germany has a seating capacity of 348, ranging from 807 (Theater am Kurfürstendamm, Berlin) to ninety (Theater in Cronenberg, Wuppertal). The boulevard comedy theatres in Bochum, Bremen, Dresden, Duisburg, Hamburg, Munich are above the average, while those in Darmstadt, Hannover, Karlsruhe, Kassel, Münster, Nürnberg-Fürth are below. Ticket prices range between €7.50 and €37. The average starting price is € 13.50, the average top price is €26.50. The price range at the Komödie im Marquardt, Stuttgart (€7.50 to €17.50) reflects the stronger subsidy this theatre enjoys, compared with the price range of the unsubsidised Komödie Düsseldorf (€13.50 to €32). All boulevard comedy theatres except Darmstadt have a subscription system in pace, which offers some reduction of seat prices. Performances at boulevard comedy theatres in Germany are scheduled for the evenings, starting at 7.30 or 8.00 p.m. and matinees on Saturdays at 5.00 p.m. Some theatres do not have performances on Mondays (Theater and der Kö, Düsseldorf) or Tuesdays (Komödie Kassel, Boulevard Münster).[10]

To summarise: boulevard comedy theatres in Germany have their characteristic ambience; their artistic managers have distinctive career patterns and there are conventions of organization, including management sharing, casting policies, touring and seat price structures, typical to boulevard comedy theatres.

Notes

1 Information based on archive research at Komödie Düsseldorf 9 April 2001.

2 Information based on archive research at Komödie Düsseldorf, 9 April 2001.

3 Information based on archive research at Boulevard Münster, 29 October 2003.

4 Unless indicated otherwise, the biographical material on Braut and Höckmann is found in program brochure No. 5, 1997/98, as researched at the theatre's archive, 9 April 2001.

5 This is Braut's opinion, as expressed in the program brochure No. 5, 1997/8, 24.

6 The culture administration of Bremen withdrew its funding from the Waldau Theater at the end of December 2003: the theatre declared bankruptcy and continued its business under insolvency regulations. In October 2004, it was taken over by Susanne and Klaus Marth, two actors in the theatre's company, who renamed the theatre 'Marth's im Waldau'. They work without subsidies and want to focus their attention on reviving theatre in the regional dialect, which was what the Waldau Theater had been famous for before being expanded into a boulevard comedy theatre.

7 Neil Simon's *Sonny Boys* turned out to be successful only when the cast included two local stars. When one of them had to be replaced for one week during the production's run due to illness, hardly any seats were sold at all [Gerd Schlesselmann, interview with the author, 4 April 2001].

8 Information based on research in the theatre's archive.

9 Both reference works, such as *Who's Who in Contemporary World Theater* (2002: 15) and *Knaurs Großer Schauspielführer* (1985: 50), highlight this characteristic of Ayckbourn's plays, as do monographs analyzing his plays, such as Paul Allen, *A pocket guide to Alan Ayckbourn's plays*, London: Faber, 2004.

10 Information based on the theatres' websites, see appendix 1.

Chapter Two

The Repertory of Boulevard Comedy Theatres in Germany

The boulevard comedy theatres in Germany have annual programs of between four and eight full-length productions. Taken together, the twenty-four boulevard comedy theatres in Germany produce more than 100 plays per year. This figure demonstrates the need for a considerable pool of plays to draw from in order to create a lively and varied repertory for the season. That pool certainly exists and can be traced back to the origins of boulevard comedy in France. French authors include classics of boulevard comedy by Labiche, Sardou, Feydeau, Bernard, Géraldy, Deval, Achard and Roussin. Marceau, Marc Camoletti (1923-2003), Barillet and Grédy, Dorin and Françoise Sagan continue this line: they represent the second generation of French writers of boulevard comedy, while Francis Veber, Schmitt, Reza and Pierre Sauvil epitomise the current generation. British authors include Travers, Noel Coward (1899-1973), Arthur Watkyn (1907-1965), Bill Naughton (1910-1992), William Douglas Home (1912-1992), Derek Benfield (b. 1926), Peter Shaffer (b.1926), Michael Pertwee, John Chapman (b. 1927), Peter Yeldham (b. 1927), Donald Churchill (1930-1991), Ray Cooney, Terence Frisby (b. 1932), Alan Ayckbourn, Simon Williams (b. 1946) and Debbie Isitt (b. 1966). American authors include Brandon Thomas (1850-1915), Mary Chase (1907-1981), Norman Krasna (1909-1984), Jerome Chodorov (b. 1911), Richard Baer (b. 1917), Leonard Gershe (1922-2002), William Goodheart (1925-1999), Neil Simon (b. 1927), Bernard Slade (b. 1930), Sam Bobrick (b. 1932), Ken Ludwig (b. 1950) and Hindi Brooks. German authors include Curt Goetz (1888-1960), Curth Flatow (b. 1920), Loriot (b. 1923 as Bernhard Victor Christoph Carl von Bülow), Horst Pillau (b. 1932), Folker Bohnet (b. 1937), Barbara Capell (b. 1949), Gunther Beth (b. 1945), Sabine Thiesler (b. 1957), Frank Pinkus (b. 1959), René Heinersdorff (b. 1963), Lars Albaum (b. 1967), Dietmar Jacobs (b. 1967), Dirk Böhling (b. 1968) and Stefan Vögel (b. 1969).

Here are a number of representative seasons at some of Germany's boulevard comedy theatres: The 2003/2004 season in Berlin included Neil

Simon's *Dinner Party*, directed by Jürgen Wölffer; Michèle Bernier and Marie Pascale Osterrieth's *Le Démon de midi* (Men and Other Errors) adapted from the cartoon by Florence Gestac, directed by Manfred Langner and *Klassentreffen* (Class Reunion), by Claus Chatten, directed by Martin Woelffer. The season continued with the world premiere of Stefan Vögel's *Süßer die Glocken* (Sweeter the Bells), directed by Folke Braband; Brandon Thomas's *Charley's Aunt*, directed by Folke Braband; due to popular demand a re-run of Vögel's *Eine Gute Partie*, starring and directed by Wolfgang Spier and Curth Flatow's *Nachspiel...Oder: Das Ende einer ersten Ehe* (Sequel / Afterplay…or: The End of a First Marriage), starring and directed by Herbert Herrmann. In addition to this main program and similar to other boulevard comedy theatres in Germany, assorted short-run extras were are also included.

The opening season of the Komödie am Altstadtmarkt, Braunschweig, included eight productions: Francis Veber's *Le Diner de cons* (The Dinner Game), directed by the theatre's artistic director, Florian Battermann; Marc Camoletti's *Boeing-Boeing*, directed by Jens Bodinus, with Battermann in the cast; *My Fat Friend* by Charles Laurence, directed by Jens Bodinus, with Battermann in the cast; *Das Traumpaar des Jahres* (The Dream Couple of the Year), written and directed by Gerd Neubert, who led the cast in *Le Diner de cons* and *My Fat Friend*; Peter Yeldham's *Birds on the Wing*, Curth Flatow's *Verlängertes Wochenende* (Extended Weekend), directed by Bodinus; a selection of sketches by Loriot, directed by Battermann; and Battermann's production of *Wann wird's mal wieder richtig Sommer* (When Are We Going to Have a Proper Summer Again?), written by Fernando Conti, a loose plot, set on a camping ground, serving as pretext for presenting a cheerful mixture of German pop songs of the 1970s.

The 2003/4 season at the Theater am Dom, Cologne, began with a transfer from Bonn's boulevard comedy theatre, Contra Kreis Theater, the world premiere production of *Einmal nicht Aufgepasst* (Careless Only Once), which the authors, Lars Albaum and Dietmar Jacobs wrote specially for the main actor, Jochen Busse, a well-known comedy actor, comedian and cabaret star. Wolfgang Spier doubled as actor and director in his production of Richard Baer's *Vermischte Gefühle* (Mixed Feelings), followed by *Willkommen im Club* (Welcome to the Club), a holiday comedy by Barbara Capell and Gunther Beth and concluded by a revival of a 2002/3 production at the *Theater an der Kö*, *Heimwerker* (D.I.Y.ers) by René Heinersdorff, Frank Hörner and Ulrich Eick-Kerssenbrock, directed by Frank Hörner.

At the TAP Komödie Darmstadt, the 2002/3 season consisted of *romance.com* by Hindi Brooks, Ray Cooney's *Caught in the Net: Run for your Wife, Again*, Pierre Sauvil's *Soleil pour deux* (Sun for Two) and Derek Benfield's *A Toe in the Water*.

A typical season for the Theater an der Kö, Düsseldorf is that of 2003/4: it started off with *Willkommen im Club* (Welcome to the Club), a holiday comedy by Barbara Capell and Gunther Beth, followed by Ayckbourn's *Relatively Speaking*, directed by René Heinersdorff, the theatre's artistic manager. It was followed by *Alles Liebe* (With Love…), written and directed by Heinersdorff, a transfer from Bonn's boulevard comedy theatre, Contra Kreis Theater, the world premiere production of *Einmal nicht Aufgepasst* (Careless only Once), which the authors, Lars Albaum and Dietmar Jacobs wrote specially for the main actor, Jochen Busse, a well-known comedy actor, comedian and cabaret star. The season also included the world premiere of Peter H Jamin's *Bestseller*, directed by Heinersdorff, with a major television star and his equally well-known son playing father and son; and a revival of Munich's Kleine Komödie am Max II production (another world premiere), *Alles Böse zum Geburtstag* (All bad Wishes for your Birthday), by Folker Bohnet and Alexander Alexy. In addition, there were a series of one-off shows, usually taken from the touring circuit in Germany and shown in between the two-month runs of the major productions.

At the Neues Theater Hannover, the plays of the 2003/4 season were Neil Simon's *The Last of the Red Hot Lovers*, directed by the theatre's artistic manager, James von Berlepsch, which was revived at the end of the season because of its enormous box office success, Patrick Barlow's *The Messiah*, Laurence Roman's *Alone Together* and Curt Goetz, *Hokuspokus*, starring James von Berlepsch and directed by a protégé of the house, Florian Battermann, since 2003 artistic manager at his own boulevard comedy theatre, *Komödie am Altstadtmarkt* in Braunschweig.

The 2003/4 season is a typical example of the Komödie Kassel: it started off with Ray Cooney's *Caught in the Net: Run for your Wife, Again*, followed, in turn, by the first German production of Pierre Sauvil's *La Surprise* (The Surprise), directed by artistic manager Roland Heitz; Tony Dunham's *Heartland*; a crime thriller, Ira Levin's *Veronica's Room*; Derek Benfield's *Don't Lose the Place*; Alfred Uhry's *Driving Miss Daisy*; the world premiere of Pierre Franckh's *Das ist mein Bett* (That's my Bed) and *Ich will Spaß, oder: Wo bitte ist die Fernbedinung* (I want Fun, or: Where, please, is the remote control?) by Dirk Böhling. In the previous season, the predecessor of this production showed the Wöhlermann family in a revue of the 1970s. Its popular success led to the commissioning of the sequel, dealing with the 1980s.

In the 2003/2004 season the Boulevard Münster showed four productions: Claude Magnier's *Monsieur Masure* (A Clear-Cut Case), directed by artistic manager Angelika Ober, who also performs a minor part, design by Peter Pittermann; John Chapman's *It Started at Harrods*, directed by Andreas Kaufmann, who regularly directs at the Boulevard Münster, design by Elke Ober and with Angelika Ober in the cast; Laurence Roman's *Make me a Match*, directed by another *Boulevard Münster* regular, Gert Becker, design by Pittermann, with Angelika Ober in the cast; and *Die 8 Millionäre* (The 8 Millionaires) by Robert Thomas, directed by Natasha Kalmbach, designed by Elke Ober. There are two performances on New Year's Eve, traditionally in Germany a popular evening for attending the theatre and three separate performances of *Dinner for One* in the afternoon, the stage version of a television program that is repeated every year on New Year's Eve, a unique phenomenon in Germany.

At the Komödie im Marquardt, Stuttgart, the 2000/2001 season consisted of Curth Flatow's *Keine Ehe nach Maß* (An Unconventional Marriage), Horst Pillau's *Jessica kommt zurück* (Jessica Returns), Ken Ludwig's *Lend me a Tenor*, Frank Pinkus' *Zurück zum Happy End* (Back to the Happy Ending), and *Oh Sippschaft* (Oh Family), an evening with two comedies by Ludwig Thoma, in a version by Johann Martin Enderle in the local, Swabian dialect. The choice of plays is characteristic for the *Komödie im Marquardt*: German authors such as Curth Flatow and Pillau, pure farce of the 'open door, close door' variety with *Lend me a Tenor* and the specialty of the Komödie im Marquardt, a play rendered in Swabian dialect. A few seasons back, Enderle wrote a Swabian version of Goethe's *Mitschuldigen* (Accomplices) and the production had a locally well-known actor in the leading role. Artistic manager Elert Bode also emphasised new plays, presenting a number of world premieres of plays by Horst Pillau and a special feat was the world premiere of Stefan Vögel's *Eine Gute Partie* (Check, Mate), which has been taken up at almost all the other boulevard comedy theatres in Germany since.

For 2004, five major productions were staged at the Theater in Cronenberg (TiC), Wuppertal: *The Woman Who Cooked Her Husband*, a farce by Debbie Isitt, Paul Pörtner's *Shear Madness*, a crime comedy with audience participation, *Fleur de Cactus* (The Cactus Flower) by Barillet and Grédy, a selection of sketches by German writer Loriot and *Pension Schöller* by Carl Laufs und Wilhelm Jacoby. In addition, there was a range of cabaret shows, revues and chanson evenings.

Only a small number of the plays in the German boulevard comedy theatre's repertories have attracted academic writing or popularity beyond the confines of the boulevard comedy theatre scene. They include Alan Ayckbourn and Neil Simon from Britain and the United States of America, respectively. Curt Goetz is a popular dramatist in Germany, no least because he starred in and directed film versions of some of the plays he wrote; German television frequently repeats the films. German readers may know Loriot, the pen name of Victor von Bülow. He became famous across Germany through a series of television shows in which he presented sketches he wrote and performed himself and from two full-length films he wrote, acted in and directed and from several books he published, which are based on and expanding his sketches. Pierre Barillet and Jean-Pierre Grédy may be known, at least indirectly, because their play *Fleur de Cactus* was made into a film starring Audrey Hepburn and Walter Matthau. However, most of the writers of boulevard comedy in Germany are not widely known beyond the limited number of boulevard comedy theatre audiences and have been ignored by academia. This chapter bridges that obvious gap, focusing on the plays of the most well known and commercially successful, active German writer of boulevard comedy, Curth Flatow in comparison with the wider field of the boulevard comedy theatre repertory.

The Set

There is some truth in Bode's ironic assertion that conventionally, as far as the set is concerned, boulevard comedy theatre presents an image of better, more beautiful interior design.[1] Indeed, when the curtain opens for performances at boulevard comedy theatres, the set on stage conventionally shows the interior of a house: a living room, a bedroom, a kitchen, or a combination of those spaces. These rooms are beautiful to look at because they are elegantly furnished in pleasing colours. The design, the furniture and the fabrics used to create this impression of beauty suggest that the owners of that house or flat are members of at least the middle classes. Audiences looking at a beautiful set feel pleased, 'at home' and comfortable. Thus, if the set is beautiful it fulfils its purposes specific to boulevard comedy theatre: to contribute to a pleasant and entertaining ambience of the performance that lacks confrontational potential. Many of the characters in German boulevard comedy are well established middle-class characters, the kind of people who also make up the majority of the German boulevard comedy theatre audiences: medical doctors, teachers, various kinds of civil servants and public sector workers, nurses, actors, musicians and writers. For example, for the set of *Gesegnetes Alter* (Blessed Age, 1996), Flatow explicitly states, in the stage directions at the beginning of the play that the room we see is upper middle class.

Ein gutbürgerliches, etwas altmodisch eingerichtetes Wohnzimmer. Ganz links führt eine Tür zu einer Terrasse, die man auch von einem anderen Zimmer aus erreichen kann, dessen Tür wir nicht sehen. Rechts neben der Terrassentür befindet sich ein Fenster. An der hinteren Wand steht ein alter Schrank mit Glastüren, der bis obenhin mit Meißner Porzellan gefüllt ist. Dahinter führt eine Tür zu den anderen Zimmern. Vor dem Fenster eine Sitzgruppe mit Sofa. Fast in der Mitte des Zimmers ein Schreibtisch—auch mehrere Jahrzehnte alt—auf dem sich ein Telefon mit Anrufbeantworter befindet. Die Nachrichten, die die Anrufer auf das Gerät sprechen, sind immer sehr laut zu hören, da der Wohnungseigentümer schon etwas schwerhörig ist. Neben dem Telefon steht ein Kassettenrekorder mit Mikrophon. Dahinter ein Schränkchen mit mehreren Schubladen, ein Regal, in dem ein paar Bücher stehen, ganz rechts an der Tür, die zur Diele führt, eine Art Vertiko mit Schubladen. Darauf ein nagelneuer Fernsehapparat. Die rechte Wand reicht nicht ganz bis nach vorn, so daß wir die Wohnungstür sehen können. Das Zimmer ist ausgesprochen reichlich möbliert. Auch im Durchgang steht ein Schränkchen mit mehreren Schubladen. Es muß alles ein wenig verwahrlost aussehen. Auf einem der Schränkchen steht ein großes, gerahmtes Foto seiner Frau. (2)
[An upper middle class, somewhat old-fashioned living room. On the very left a door leads to a balcony, which can be reached from one other room, whose door we cannot see. On the right next to the balcony door there is a window. On the back wall there is an old wardrobe with glass doors and it is filled to the top with Meissner porcelain. Behind this, a door leads to the other rooms. In front of the window is an arrangement of armchairs with a sofa. Almost in the middle of the room there is a desk, also several decades old, on which there is a telephone with an answerphone. The messages that callers leave on this answerphone can always be heard at a very loud volume because the owner of the flat is a bit hard of hearing. Next to the telephone stands a tape recorder with microphone. Behind that a little cupboard with several drawers, a shelf on which there are a couple of books and all the way on the right by the door that leads to the hall, a kind of cabinet with drawers. On top of that a brand new television. The right hand wall does not extend all the way to the front so that we can see the entrance door. The room is very densely furnished. Also in the passage way is a little cupboard with several drawers. Everything has to look a little untidy and run down. On one of the chests of drawers there is a large framed photo of the owner's wife.]

For the spectators, a wardrobe with glass doors filled with valuable Meissner china represents a specific pointer to that class. According to the stage directions, the wardrobe is to be placed against the back wall: it is thus in full view of the spectators, allowing them to pick up the pointer easily.

The interior space on stage is most often characteristic of the people who live there. In *Gesegnetes Alter*, the main character, Georg Neumann, has just celebrated his ninetieth birthday. In line with his age, Flatow points out that the room is old-fashioned, with furniture that must have been very elegant when new, but now shows clear signs of age and wear and tear. Felix Rombach, the main character of Flatow's *Zweite Geige* (Second Fiddle, 1991), is a happy and cheerful chap. He has a nice, cosy flat, a secure job as second violinist in the orchestra of the municipal theatre, a very motherly housekeeper and frequently changing love interests among the pretty ladies from the theatre's ballet company. While much of the other information becomes apparent in the first scenes of the play, which serve the function of exposition, the set provides the first impression of the character as well: the space itself is not too large, the furniture is somewhat nondescript, lacks originality, is neither antique nor modern, but very comfortable for its owner.[2] The main character in Flatow's *Der Mann, der sich nicht traut...* (Happy Wedding, 1973), Wolfgang Jäger, a divorced single parent, has arranged his life very meticulously. Apart from clear pointers in the plot, such as the revelation that he entertains a once-a-week relationship with his secretary, the set enhances his pedantic nature such as to make it obvious for the audience: in the second scene of the play the spectators see Jäger finish vacuum-cleaning; he places the vacuum cleaner in front of the broom cupboard and presses a button. The cupboard door opens and the vacuum cleaner is pulled into the broom cupboard, whose doors close automatically, all accompanied by the noise emitted by an electric winch once he has pressed the button (1973: 1). Later in the same scene, he checks the table his son has carefully laid for breakfast and rearranges it, commenting while he does so:

> Die Tasse steht auf einer Kaffeeuntertasse, in der Butter steckt das Käsemesser, die Zuckerdose gehört zu dem guten Geschirr, die Eierlöffel glänzen durch Abwesenheit, und die Teelöffel glänzen überhaupt nicht—die hast du gestern abgewaschen ... (*er bringt rasch alles in Ordnung*). (13)
> [The teacup is on a coffee saucer. The knife in the butter is a cheese knife, the sugar pot is part of the good porcelain, the egg spoons are missing and the teaspoons are blunt—you did the dishes yesterday, I believe. (*he quickly puts all in order*)]

When Julia, the woman he had fallen in love with, leaves Jäger, he is desperate and this shows in the state of the room when the curtain rises on the first scene after the play's interval: his kitchen is untidy, there are piles of medicine bottles on the table and the doors to the other rooms branching off from the kitchen are open. Jäger's dark clothes, in striking contrast to the over-colourful shirt he wore in an earlier scene in the play also set in the kitchen, enhance the mood of depression carried by the appearance of the set and the music from the radio, Gluck's *Ce farò senza*, the aria showing Orpheus bemoaning his losing Eurydice, provides ironic comment on Jäger's situation.

A third characteristic of the set in boulevard comedy theatre is its functional nature. In other genres of drama, set designers have much more freedom to create from the depths of their imagination: Shakespeare's *A Midsummer Night's Dream* can be set in as realistic a wood as possible, with real soil and trees on the stage, or it can be set in a boarding school dormitory. The witches in *Macbeth* can be fairy tale creatures in a space created with stage fog and lighting effects, or they can be operating theatre assistants pushing trolleys. In boulevard comedy theatre, the set must be functional to the prime purpose of the play, to elicit laughter in the audience. This is why the dramatists writing in this genre take pains to describe the set in detail, even for a set that is easy to construct for the designer. The amount of detail thus does not correlate to the complexity of set. If the designer chooses to deviate from those instructions, the consequences for the director and the actors can be considerable. A door may have to be precisely where the dramatist requests it, or at least one humorous situation will just not be allowed to exist in the production.

Dramatists of boulevard comedy theatre do not stop at describing the basic lay-out of the set, usually at the beginning of the play script: they vary aspects of it from scene to scene, as the plot development demands. In the first scene of Flatow's *Gesegnetes Alter*, for example, the lighting on the set is to suggest mid-morning and a transparent glass bottle of medicine, half empty, is placed prominently on the table, in such a way that spectators can read part of its label: 'Lebelang' [Life/live long]. In addition, the stage directions require several bouquets and arrangements of flowers, with a golden '90' on one of them, as well as some wrapped presents and congratulation letters and cards. All these details suggest to the spectators, before they have seen any of the characters, that someone has celebrated his or her ninetieth birthday very recently. The audience is then able to establish a link between the birthday, old age and the medicine 'Live Long'. Thus Flatow's playful use of the basic set and his attention to detail allow for a first potentially humorous association in the play.³ At the end of the first scene, Georg desperately searches for something in his flat. The curtain falls and at the beginning of the second scene, when the curtain rises again, the audience is confronted with a picture of considerable chaos: Georg is on his knees, still searching. Several of the drawers from various chests of drawers have been pulled out and their contents are on the floor (15). Flatow puts this situation to comic use when Christa, a young student whom Georg has hired to help him with housework comes to introduce herself a few seconds later.

In *Der Mann, der sich nicht traut...* and *Gesegnetes Alter*, Jäger and Georg, respectively, create characteristic changes of the set themselves. A variation of this scenario occurs when a character who has made his home on his own and likes it that way has visitors, often not invited, who change everything. In *Zweite Geige*, Felix, many years ago, had the love of his life, Christa, but she had to undergo an appendix operation just when they were preparing to get married and she ended up marrying the House Officer instead. In the meantime Christa has made her husband into a renowned professor and has nothing left to do in that respect. So she remembers Felix, with whom her ambitions find much to do: he plays only second violin in the orchestra, rather than first and 'second fiddle' describes his entire life well: this needs to be changed, Christa thinks. She moves in with Felix and she rearranges all the furniture and thus destroys the comfortable feel of the room. Similarly, in *Mein Vater, der Junggeselle* (My Father the Bachelor, 1994), Thomas arrives unexpectedly and uninvited at the flat in which his father, Frank Hoffmann, has made his comfortable and spacey home since he moved out of the former family home following his divorce. Thomas brings his own possessions and later Frank's ex-wife Barbara turns up with a piano and a complete drum kit, thus making the space cramped and in the process ruining any comfort and cosiness both Frank and the audience initially associated with the space.

Telephone Conversations

Once the scene has been set, it is of course important to familiarise the audience with the characters and the situation those characters are in. Often Flatow uses a telephone conversation to convey such information, either at the beginning of a play or partway through it. In *Verlängertes Wochenende* (Extended Weekend, 1990), stewardess Karin is on the phone as the curtain rises at the beginning of the play. She talks to a friend, whom she has not talked to for a while, so she has to fill her in. The audience finds out that Karin got her divorce six months ago and has now arranged her first date since then. She is very excited. She lives together with another stewardess, Doris, who is also single, is also looking for Mr. Right and cannot find him because, as Karin puts it, 'Ich glaube der macht das Suchen viel zu viel Spaß.' (1) [I think that she enjoys searching far too much]. Flatow's *Romeo mit grauen Schläfen* (Romeo with Grey Temples, 1985) also opens with a phone conversation: in this case of the housekeeper, Frau Bethge. Smoking a cigarette, she talks about her previous employer and how her attempts to seduce him failed: when she intentionally appeared in an almost see-through nightgown, he ignored her three times and the forth time he ran to his room and locked himself in (6). While in those two plays, the persons Karin and Mrs Bethge talk to remain unseen, in *Der Mann, der sich nicht traut...* both Jäger's ex-wife, Sonja and Julia's current boyfriend, Teddy, appear at the side of the stage in spotlights for their telephone conversations with Jäger and Julia. Thus Flatow allows the spectators to find out more about those characters than would be possible, at least without becoming obvious and clumsy, by way of conversation. Sonja comes across as a fashion-crazy, shallow woman early on in the play, which prepares the spectator for her appearance later on together with other characters. Spectators see Teddy repeatedly short of small change when using public phone booths to call Julia. The play was written before the days of charge cards, credit cards and mobile phones. The clash between the information that Teddy is a pilot (whom an audience would expect to be highly organised) and the absent-mindedness he conveys in the phone call scenes, has potential for humour; a later scene takes this clash further when Teddy complies more with the macho image the audience is given in when Julia talks about him.

Efficient Scene Endings

One of the tricks of the trade in writing boulevard comedy is to find a particularly good punch line for the end of a scene, followed by a briskly closing curtain. In *Der Mann, der sich nicht traut...*, Julia and her niece Gaby have been discussing Julia's inability to attract unmarried men. Toward the end of the scene, Gaby asks whether Julia might be successful with her current lover, Teddy, if he were to get a divorce. Julia responds that she does not want to get the blame for Teddy's marriage breaking up. Gaby jokingly scolds Julie for her capriciousness: 'Beefsteak willst du essen—aber das Rind soll nicht geschlachtet werden ... (25) [You want to eat steak, but without killing the cow]. The effect of the punchline is enhanced in five different, almost concomitant ways: Gaby, who just delivered the punchline, leaves the stage, while Julia, at whose expense the punchline achieved its humour, is left on stage to react appropriately; there is an aural effect in that Gaby slams the door on leaving and there are two further visual effects: the lights black out and the curtain closes.

In the same play, Julia visits Jäger in his office to plead for him to allow Gaby and Jäger's son Ullrich to get married. Flatow plays with a number of audience expectations here. At the beginning of the scene, it is obvious how charming and attractive Jäger finds Julia. His attitude changes abruptly when he realises that she has come about his son. When Julia finds him unrelenting and gets angry, preparing to leave in a huff, Jäger becomes conciliatory, admitting that he was perhaps a bit rough in his tone, but after all, he had feared, initially, that his son wanted to marry Julia. Here he reverts to the charming behaviour she triggered in him at the beginning of the scene, suggesting to the audience that much of what went on between Jäger and Julia during the scene is some kind of battle of the sexes common to boulevard comedy. With Julia's response, 'Ach...und Sie fanden mich zu alt für ihn...' [Oh and you thought that I was too old for him?], Julia seems to pick up on Jäger's tone, which Jäger in turn carries further when he smiles and confirms her impression. He does so in such a way that allows Julia to pick up another cliché: 'Sagen Sie jetzt bloß nicht, ich könnte seine Mutter sein...' [Now don't say I could be his mother...]. She would dread that thought, she says, shuddering. Banter depends on the rule that both parties understand what the other person is saying although they pretend otherwise. Now, however, Jäger does not understand what Julia means; he has lost the momentum of his counter-attack of charming banter and responds with a nonplussed 'why?', which is the cue for Julia's punchline that ends the scene: 'Dann wäre ich ja mit Ihnen verheiratet!!!' [Because then I would be married to you!!!]. The pattern is similar to the one discussed for the end of the scene with Julia and Gaby from the same play: The person who delivers the punchline, in this case Julia, leaves. She slams the door behind her. The character at whose expense the punchline is funny, Jäger, remains behind, taken aback. The lights black out and the curtain falls.

The first scene of Samuel Taylor's *Gracious Living* (1978) shows aging former film star Donald Renshaw during a shooting session for a television advertising spot—he finds out only in the process that he has not been employed for the spot: he is only one of many at a casting call among whom the sponsor and the advertising agency will decide. He is so upset that he breaks off take after take. The crew and casting director express their gratitude that he was able to come—they will get in touch with his agent, which is the usual, polite way of saying that he was not successful and will not get the part. Donald has the final line of the scene: when the casting director mentions Donald's agent, Donald replies that it is too late to get in touch with his agent, because he just committed suicide.

Professional clichés

Flatow and other writers of boulevard comedy manage to create laughter from clichés associated with some other professions. Two examples, relating to the medical profession and to actors, are worth considering. In *Der Mann, der sich nicht traut...*, Jäger, in hospital, has himself checked by a stomach consultant. On the day of his discharge, he has a final meeting with that consultant's registrar (*Oberarzt*). Dr. Gnippig's outward appearance is in line with expectations of hospital doctors in Germany: he wears a white doctor's gown, carries patients' medical records and has a stethoscope round his neck. He talks to the grown-up patient, Jäger, as if to a child when he catches him out of bed: 'Nanu...?! Wer tanzt denn hier so fröhlich herum...? Wir sollen doch schön ruhig im Bett bleiben!... Nun aber husch, husch... ins Körbchen...!' (96-7) [Who's hopping about so happily there? We should stay in bed very nicely, shouldn't we? Off you go!] and uses the third person plural when asking 'Wie fühlen wir uns denn?' [And how are we feeling, then?]. Flatow uses the cliché for a number of humorous situations: the doctor has looked at the wrong patient's record and therefore thinks he is talking to a patient with a heart problem. Flatow here takes up the cliché that senior hospital doctors do not know their patients personally, not even to the extent that they know what they are suffering from, without reference to the medical records. When Dr. Gnippig consequently checks Jäger's heart, he is much surprised to find that it does not show any sign of illness. As he later puts it, he was worried unless their medication had actually helped the patient. In the process of the checkup, Dr Gnippig asks Jäger to inhale, exhale and stop breathing, rather ordinary requests in the context of a medical examination. The process turns to comedy when Flatow plays with the cliché of the obedient patient: Jäger, too eagerly following the doctor's orders, does not resume breathing until he almost suffocates. The doctor is alarmed: 'Was haben Sie denn...? Sie sind ja ganz rot im Gesicht! Kriegen Sie keine Luft...?' [What's the matter? You're quite red in the face. Do you have difficulties breathing?]. Another related cliché turned to comic effect is the patient taking the doctor's metaphors literally: while Dr. Gnippig listens to Jäger's heartbeat through his stethoscope, he comments: 'Nichts', referring, as the audience learns later, to the fact that he cannot hear anything wrong with the heart. Jäger misunderstands and worries that he might not have any heartbeat at all any more and almost in a panic grabs his wrist and tries to feel his pulse. A similar situation occurs soon after this in the scene: Dr. Gnippig takes the correct patient file and Jäger asks whether the two-week series of check-ups have yielded any results and whether anything can be done. The way he phrases the latter question implies that he is rather pessimistic about his state of health and fears for the worst. Dr. Gnippig answers 'nothing', implying that the doctors did not find anything wrong with him. Jäger, however, relates the 'nothing' to his second question and now assumes that he is indeed, just as he had feared, terminally ill.

Jäger's status during his two weeks in hospital is that of a private patient, a well-known concept in Germany: civil servants in this country are eligible to have half of their health costs covered by the state and the other half by private health insurance. In surgeries and in hospitals, private patients get more comprehensive, faster and more expensive treatment than patients who have to rely on the state health service. Flatow refers to this common knowledge of German audiences when Jäger complains that despite his status as a private patient, i.e., despite the fact that the hospital and the doctors who treated him received much money for their efforts, they did not find 'anything wrong' with him. Dr. Gnippig plays along with this line of comedy when he agrees that the hospital indeed subjected Jäger to all sophisticated and thus expensive procedures they could think of; the comical implication is that the doctors went to all that effort to make as much money as possible, rather than to find out what caused Jäger's stomach problems.

In *Romeo mit grauen Schläfen*, Alexander Fischer, known as Alfi, is a typical star actor. In the first scene of the play the audience sees him coming home from work. He immediately complains to his housekeeper, Frau Bethge: 'Das war heute wieder anstrengend...acht Stunden Synchron...' (10) [That was straining again today... Eight hours of dubbing.] He notices that Frau Bethge has been smoking. He tells her off for it. She suggests she open the windows. He his horrified at the idea: 'Wenn Sie wüßten, wie empfindlich meine Stimmbänder sind. Der kleinste Lufthauch genügt, schon ist die Stimme weg.' (10) [If you only knew how delicate my vocal cords are! The slightest draft of air is enough and my voice's gone already.]

A female housekeeper appears in several of Flatow's boulevard comedies, providing a solid presence in flats where many characters habitually come and go. She is also usually insistently curious. What she finds out proves useful for the spectators to learn more about the characters as well in the process. The housekeeper thus serves as another device for providing information. This character's curiosity, moreover, provides ample opportunities for laugher. In *Mein Vater, der Junggeselle*, Frank Hoffman's ex-wife, Barbara, comes to his flat unexpectedly, looking for her ex-husband. Frank's housekeeper, Frau Stadelmeyr is the only person on stage when Barbara arrives, so Barbara asks her to tell Frank that she is here to see him. Frau Stadelmeyr's curiosity shows, with her question: 'In welcher Angelegenheit?' (23) [Concerning what?] . This question elicits a harsh 'Das geht Sie gar nichts an.' [That's none of your business.] from Barbara, showing the spectators how determined and tense she is and providing a cue for a physical reaction from the actor playing Frau Stadelmeyr to this aggression from Barbara, to accompany her 'Was?' [What?] in such a way as to provoke audience laughter. Frau Stadelmeyr made it obvious earlier in that scene that she does not understand why Frank divorced his wife; now that she has seen Barbara herself and has suffered at her aggression, she leaves assuring Frank that she does understand him, after all. When Felix in *Zweite Geige* receives a letter from Christa, the major love interest in his life, his housekeeper, Frau Baumgärtner is so curious that she manages to find out all about that episode in Felix's life. The audience can laugh at her insatiable curiosity and finds out important information at the same time.

The female housekeeper in Flatow's plays is conventionally a very respectable woman, or at least that is what she thinks of herself. She likes order and regards herself as its guardian. Thus in *Mein Vater, der Junggeselle* Flatow informs the audience that Frank Hoffmann is a newspaper reporter and at one point wrote a column about the stupidest bank robber of all times, who was so much in a hurry to pack the money into his bag that he handed his gun to the teller so as to have both hands free. Towards the end of the play, that bank robber is released from prison and rings the bell to Frank's flat. He asks him outside and beats him up. Then Thomas comes out of the flat and beats up the criminal. The audience does not see this, it happens off stage. Frau Stadelmeyr opens the door to the staircase and shouts: 'Und Sie stehen jetzt sofort auf. Ich habe es gar nicht gern, wenn auf meiner Treppe etwas herumliegt.' (36) [And you can get up at once. I don't like things lying about on my stairs.]. Frau Stadelmeyr's exclamation shows both her sense for orderliness and it is funny because she refers to the huge criminal as 'things'.

After Thomas has knocked out the criminal using Karate, Frau Stadelmeyr is in awe (36). In this context, the female housekeeper tends to like, or even mother her male employer. In *Romeo mit Grauen Schläfen*, Frau

Bethge has romantic aspirations towards all her employers. In *Zweite Geige*, Flatow repeatedly emphasises how motherly Frau Baumgärtner feels towards Felix. She does not only cook and clean for him but like a mother she is used to Felix' frequent lady visitors, always a new one. When she comes to do her work and hears the current one, Eva Maria, singing in the bathroom, she comments dryly: 'Aber ich gehe wieder, irgendetwas wird schon fehlen. Das Bad kann ich ja auch noch nicht machen.'(25) [But I am going again. Something's bound to be missing. I can't clean the bathroom yet anyway, I guess']. When Christa moves in with Felix and turns the entire flat on its head, Frau Baumgärtner resigns. However, she is unable to stay away because of her motherly attachment to Felix. Like a mother, she knows her 'son' and helps him: she realises and makes Felix realise, that he has really, genuinely fallen in love with Silvi, the daughter of Christa and her husband, Professor Rademacher. In the end Felix is happily back to normal and that means, on that day, Eva Maria. Frau Baumgärtner has the final lines of the play

> Frau Baumgärtner: Ich wollte Sie nur fragen, es ist Ihnen sicher recht, wenn ich morgen etwas später komme.
> Felix: Es ist mir recht. Bis morgen Frau Baumgärtner.
> Eva Maria: Tschau.
> Frau Baumgärtner: Dann gehe ich jetzt. (guckt zu Eva Maria) Sie haben ja alles was Sie brauchen.
> *(Felix guckt nacheinander zu beiden und nickt dann)* (146)
> [Frau Baumgärtner: I just wanted to ask you, it is surely ok with you if I come a little later tomorrow.
> Felix: That's ok. See you tomorrow, Frau Baumgärtner
> Eva Maria: Ciao.
> Frau Baumgärtner: Well, I'll be off then. *(Looks at Eva Maria)* You have got everything you need.
> *(Felix looks at both in turn and nods)]*

No matter how amorous or motherly the female housekeeper tends to feel for her male employer, the employers address her and the audience thus knows her, only by her last name, indicative that ultimately she keeps her distance to her usually male employer, or at least that such distance is maintained by the males she serves.

When writers of boulevard comedy employ professional clichés to create humorous situations or dialogues, they take for granted some audience knowledge about the chosen profession. Doctors appear most frequently: the main character in *Fleur de Cactus* by Barillet and Grédy is a dentist and the plot involves his assistant. Gunther Philipp's *Da wird Daddy Staunen* (Daddy Will Be Surprised) is also placed squarely in the milieu of doctors—perhaps not surprisingly, because before Philipp (1918-2004) embarked on a long and successful career as actor and writer, he studied and practiced medicine, specializing in neurology. The main character of the play, George Ashley, is professor of human genetics and has been asked by the World Health Organization to take on a project promoting birth control in Africa. While he is away for months, his wife gives birth to twins—not the ideal publicity for Ashley, who is due to receive a knighthood, so everyone tries to hide the event from him and the public. His mentor, Dr. Peter Morris (a part Philipp wrote for himself) and his assistant, Dr. Berny Bedford, get involved in the plot. Stanley Price's *The Starving Rich* is set in a beauty farm where fat rich people hope to slim down; Patricia Levrey's *A cloche pied* (Break a Leg) is set in a hospital, where CEO Dany Clement recovers from a major motorbike accident. Used to run her own advertising agency, her family and her circle of friends, she turns her room in the hospital into a place where fellow patients come for counselling and alternative advice, to the concern of the medical staff, represented in the play by the consultant and the sister in charge.

Horst Pillau accumulates four professional clichés in one play: *Guten Tag, Herr Liebhaber* (Good Morning, Mr. Lover, 1997) is about tax inspector Georg Liebhaber and his superior, Hilmar Peters. They carry out a tax audit of famous film director Lisa Bach, who is regularly visited by her mother, Viola and is capably supported by her assistant, Ossie Potmann. Lisa is a career woman and a kind of diva, extravagant but hiding some loneliness underneath her glamorous outside. Georg is a typical civil servant, stiff and formal, hiding whatever human sides he may have behind paragraphs from tax law. For example, when he finally kisses Lisa for the first time, she sighs with relief and asks him to finally say her name, 'Nicht sachlich. Nicht streng. Sondern ganz zärtlich. Liebevoll. Süß.' (65) [Not matter-of-factly. Not sternly. But very tenderly. Lovingly. Sweetly.]. Georg embraces her, kisses her again and says very lovingly: '304…slash 25965…dash 95.' It is her tax reference number and with this punch line the audience is sent into the play's interval. The older tax inspector, Hilmar, ends up in mutual love with Viola and Georg with Lisa. Ossie knows hundreds of people and their phone numbers by heart and is always on the phone arranging things. His hyperactivity compensates, however, for a difficult life with his severely disabled adult daughter.

Samuel Taylor uses the cliché of the fading film star, Renshaw, in his *Gracious Living*. While at the casting call for a television commercial,

Renshaw immediately notices that the spotlight is on the pack of painkillers he has to hold up, rather than fully on himself and tries to have this changed. When his efforts fail, he moves himself almost imperceptibly into the centre of the spotlight. Later in the play, he is given the part of Polonius in a stage production of Shakespeare's *Hamlet*, in which a rock star plays Hamlet and Renshaw's wife plays Gertrude. In a central scene in the play, following the opening night, the Renshaws and their agent read the newspaper reviews, which are devastating for Renshaw, because he improvised much of the text and instead of having himself killed by Hamlet behind the arras, he jumped out from behind the arras and had a major sword duel with Hamlet before allowing Hamlet to kill him. Dying Polonius walked off stage with the words of Horatio, 'Good night, sweet prince.' The audience applauded on his exit, Renshaw remembers proudly. His wife retorts that they were applauding because they were so relieved to be rid of him. She observed the audience: John Gielgud had tears streaming down his cheeks and Laurence Olivier stuffed a handkerchief into his mouth to prevent himself from bursting out laughing.

Service staff appears regularly in boulevard comedy, for example Berthe in Camoletti's *Boeing-Boeing*. She is aware of the three girlfriends her employer, Bernard, has at the same time and comments, on one occasion, that such a house is really not an ideal workplace for a decent maid, especially since she always had top marks in religious education at school.

The Generation Gap

One of the sources of laughter in German boulevard comedy is the generation gap. Flatow, for example, uses it in *Mein Vater, der Junggeselle*. Thomas turns up at his father Frank's flat unexpectedly for breakfast, complete with suitcases, to move in with him. He comments on the beautiful woman whom he has just seen in the staircase. Frank and the audience know that he is referring to Cornelia, Frank's new girl friend, with whom he has just spent the night and whom he asked to leave so that Thomas would not see her in his flat. Thomas now wonders whether his father is still physically capable of a sexual relationship, because he finds him too thin and lacking energy. He promises to make sure, from now on, that his father will get enough to eat (15). Thomas also comments on his father's dressing gown: 'Den Dressing Gown kannst du auch vergessen. Gehört in die Altkleidersammlung.' (14) [Forget about that dressing gown, it belongs in a collection of old clothes]. Here Thomas, representing the young generation, has problems with his father's tastes, representing the older generation.

In Flatow's *Der Mann, der sich nicht traut...*, the roles are reversed. Jäger is a man in his late forties. He considers himself progressive and is concerned how conservative his son has turned out. For their first scene together in the play, the stage directions describe Jäger wearing an outrageously colourful shirt, whereas his son Ullrich wears grey and black trousers and shirt. Their conversation constitutes a banter around that difference: Jäger starts off looking his son up and down and commenting: 'Hübsch siehst du aus...So Ton in Ton...und so fröhliche Farben...! Du könntest ein buntes Hemd tragen!...' (12) [You look smart. Such matching and cheery colours. You could possibly wear a more colourful shirt.] Ullrich retorts that Jäger would have to struggle hard to find a more colourful shirt than the one he is wearing now. Jäger response suggests that they have had that kind of exchange before. He takes the shirt off to put it into the washing machine, asking Ullrich for permission to put on the shirt he takes out of the dryer. Ullrich indicates that he has given that shirt to Jäger as a present, which reminds Jäger that he wanted to exchange it for a different one when he received it from his son.

Their banter turns into a more serious confrontation later in the same scene of the play, after Jäger refuses to give his permission to Ullrich and his fiancée Gaby to get married. Ullrich accuses Jäger of being more like a dictator than a father. Jäger complains that he has to hear such inappropriate words from his son on an empty stomach. Ullrich threatens to move out of the flat they share, a threat, Jäger's response suggests, that Ullrich has made before, without acting on it. Jäger in turn repeats his claim that Ullrich could never find a better place to live, especially since every Tuesday, when Jäger has his once-a-week date with his secretary, Ullrich has the flat for himself to be with his girl friends. Ullrich gets even more vexed at this repetition, accusing his father of not knowing anything about true love. Jäger angrily calls his son an old-fashioned petit bourgeois, an accusation Ullrich returns with 'Und du hältst dich wohl für sehr jung—dabei bist du uralt...' (19-20) [And you think you are young, don't you—wrong: you're past it]. Outraged, Jäger shows his son that he is still able to bend down with straight knees and touch the floor with his finger tips. Ullrich laughs at this, commenting, depending on whether the actor who plays Jäger is short or tall: 'Kunststück, bei deinen kurzen Beinen / bei deinen Affenarmen' ((19-20) [No wonder, with your short legs / monkey arms...]

Flatow's *Romeo mit grauen Schläfen* provides an interesting variation: it shows father and daughter in a dispute.[4] Here Alfi's daughter Vicky has just come back after two years away and she brings her baby boy with her, whom Alfi has not seen yet. Alfi is critical of the child's father, Felix. He was in his third term of studying sociology when Alfi last saw Vicky. He is still in his third term two years later. Vicky's explanation of this blatant lack of progress, that Felix had to take a break for while because he had broken his foot, does not impress Alfie, who asks cynically whether Felix broke his foot because he fell over his long hair. Vicky tries to speak up for Felix, explaining to Alfi that he is a very sensitive man, the first one who really took care of her very thoroughly. Alfi responds with a glance at the baby and comments 'Das sieht man' (17) [That's obvious].

In the same play Alfi tells Vicky that he is expecting a colleague and will, therefore, not have much time for her that evening. In the German original, Alfi's choice of words implies that the colleague is male. In the end, the colleague is a pretty young female starlet. Challenged by Vicky, Alfi admits that he tried to hide this detail from her, asking whether it is all that important whether the colleague is male of female. Vicky retorts that the difference is indeed important, but mainly so for Alfi himself (26). Alfi agrees with a smile and Flatow makes sure Vicky maintains the upper hand by providing her with a punch line for her exit: Frau Bethge has cooked a meal for Alfi and his lady friend and Vicky had eaten much of her share of it. So when she leaves she refers to the starlet's very young age: 'Dann werde ich ihr lieber noch was übrig lassen. Die ist ja noch im Wachstum.' (26) [I'd better leave her something then, she is still growing].

Flatow's use of the generation gap to create laughter is not restricted to members of the same family. In *Gesegnetes Alter*, ninety-year-old Georg has asked the student Christa to help him with the housework. He finds her very attractive, especially because she is wearing a mini-skirt. When Christa leaves the room to inspect the kitchen, he admits to himself how attracted he is to her sexually, despite his advanced age (18). When Christa asks him, a little later, whether he is really ninety, he points out that he has documents to prove his age, adding that she should not expect sexual harassment at her work place from him (18).

The generation gap features prominently across boulevard comedy. In Stefan Vögel's *Eine Gute Partie*, the main character, Fred Kowinski, is seventy years old and has been a widower for six years. His daughter has been living in Australia since she married the first man who came her way who was living in the Australian bush and can throw a boomerang, as Fred maliciously puts it. He is Sidney from Sydney. Fred does not see much of his daughter and appears to be bitter about this and about her choices in life. Fred's son, Leonard, did not turn out to be a rich and famous heart surgeon either and Fred feels he wasted all the money spent on Leonard's education, only for Leonard to drop out of school and become a sales representative for a vacuum cleaner company. In Fred's eyes, Leonard is a failure and he and other characters in the play poke much fun with repeated jokes regarding this profession, which indeed tends to be much ridiculed, even despised in Germany. On one occasion, for example, Leonard tries very hard to find out from his father whether he had a relationship with the housekeeper Leonard employed for his father. Other characters comically misunderstand Leonard's insistence as insistence of the sales rep selling a vacuum cleaner to his own father.

Pierre Sauvil's *Soleil pour deux* plays further on the generation gap, with the exchanges between established doctor and bachelor Dr. Bertholin and young, independent, eccentric Josiane Desrumeaux. She jumps into Dr. Bertholin's house through the window, claiming to be an ex-patient whom he diagnosed wrongly and says that she has come to blackmail him into giving her room and board for an indefinite time. Later she reveals herself to be his daughter. In Sauvil's *La Surprise* it is extravagant and extraordinary student Virginie Dumesnil who brings new life into the run-down marriage of Catherine and Philippe Chabrier. Denis Diderot, the main character in *Le Libertin* by Eric-Emmanuel Schmitt, finds himself challenged by the younger generation in the shape of his own daughter and the daughter of his current host. His daughter asks him to condone her unmarried relationship with an older man for the sole purpose or procreation and his host's daughter tries to seduce him. In this situation it is not easy for him to complete his encyclopaedia with the last remaining entry: on morals.

The generation gap is also prominent in Horst Pillau's *Mein Vater der Wessi* (My Father from West Germany, 2001). The plot takes place soon after the fall of the Wall separating East and West Germany. Student Christoph Berger suddenly appears at the house of wealthy but stressed building contractor Bruno Zweiling, explaining that he is Bruno's son from a liaison many years in the past and that his mother has just died. Bruno is living with his very young and attractive second wife, Greet. Predictably, Christoph falls in love with his new stepmother and she with him. He starts up a very successful dot.com company and turns into the stressed businessman, who ends up not having time to be with Greet—she turns to Bruno's former business partner for love. Bruno also changes his life, sells his share in the contracting business, becomes a student and starts a relationship with Sandra, who is none other than Christoph's former girlfriend.

The generation gap in a constellation of characters beyond the family is evident in Horst Pillau's *Nur noch Ausatmen* (Only Exhale, 1990). In this play, the main character is an old woman who is very active in environmental protest campaigns of all kinds, including one of her own invention: smashing up cars parked along the streets. She brings her tenant into (moral) difficulties because he is a policeman.

Couples as Central Characters

Heterosexual couples in various stages of their relationship are at the centre of many of the plays in the repertoire of German boulevard comedy theatres. Flatow actually enjoys showing the couples in his plays in bed—never fully naked, but pleasant in shape, leaving it to the audience's imagination to fill in what they cannot see. His stage directions repeatedly emphasise the need for discretion and the need for appeal. Some female characters are described as *appetitlich*, appetizing or delicious and the spectators get an impression of this when these female characters go for a shower, on their own, thus further supporting the elegant nature of eros in Flatow's plays.

In *Der Mann, der sich nicht traut...*, Jäger wakes up one morning and has difficulty realizing where he is. This furnishes much material for comedy. Waking up is shown from various perspectives: Jäger does not remember where he is, but is very pleased once he does remember—he has spent the night with Julia. Julia emerges from sleep in an unexpected (and therefore comical) way, with her head at the foot end of the bed. The explanation follows immediately and is worth quoting in full to serve as an example of Flatow's witty dialogue

> Julia *(verschlafen)*: Suchst du etwas Bestimmtes...? *(nimmt sicht die Watte aus den Ohren)*
> Jäger *(verblüfft)*: Wieso bist du denn da unten...?
> Julia *(während sie ihre Position wechselt)*: Weil oben kein Platz mehr war...Erst hast du mir die Decke weggezogen...dann hast du dich quer gelegt...(54)
> [Julia: *(dozy)* Are you looking for something in particular? *(takes cotton wool out of her ears)*
> Jäger: *(surprised)* Why are you down there?
> Julia: *(while she changes her position)* Because there was no more space up there. First you pulled the cover away from me, then you lay across the bed.]

Not only does the waking up cause laughter in both cases; it also reveals something about the falling asleep and the sleep itself: Jäger, the divorcee of eight years, usually sleeps alone and, true to habit, uses all the blanket and space available. Julia, living in an flat in the entry lane, needs cotton wool to be able to sleep and is flexible enough to work around Jäger's habits in her attempt to find space for herself in the bed. Jäger reveals an additional characteristic of his sleeping: once he wakes up he usually has a full memory of falling asleep. On this occasion, however, he suggests to Julia, it is different. Julia suspects he may have forgotten what happened before they fell asleep: ... wie du eingeschlafen bist...? (54) [How you fell asleep?] If the actor playing Julia delivers this line in an appropriately sharp tone, it is sure to create laughter in the audience, especially since they assume Jäger does remember, given the fact that he is so visibly happy when he remembers where he is. Jäger's response to Julia's suspicion that he may have forgotten how they ended up in bed together reveals a dramatic device: the audience needs to know what happened since the end of the last scene.

In a different scene in the same play Flatow shows, to comical effect, another character forced to wake up suddenly. Fräulein Lamm, Jäger's secretary, appears in a spotlight on one side of the stage, in tears and calls his home at six o'clock in the morning after he has not come over to her place the evening before as expected. Jäger is not at home—he is at Julia's place—and Ullrich enters completely dozy and with tousled hair. He mumbles angrily, complaining to himself that it's still in the middle of the night—not even six o'clock yet (51). It causes laughter when Ullrich refers to the time of 6 a.m. as the middle of the night and the actor playing Ullrich can present both the physical attributes of doziness and tousled hair and Ullrich' grumpiness when talking to Fräulein Lamb, to further comic effect. According to the stage directions, Ullrich wears only his pyjama trousers and when his fiancé Gaby joins him, equally dozy, dressed only in his pyjama top, the audience can easily infer that they have spent the night together as well, just as Jäger and Julia.

Flatow's *Mein Vater, der Junggeselle* carries the subtitle *Fast eine Bettgeschichte* [Nearly a Bed Story]. The play starts with a couple in bed. There is a clear parallel here to the scene in *Der Mann der sich nicht traut...* discussed above. Just as with that earlier play, Flatow creates laughter from the way he shows the female character, Cornelia's tiredness when waking up. Once both she and Frank are sufficiently awake, however, they engage in witty banter, which serves the function of exposition. However, information is not provided in a straightforward manner, but with misleading sentences that cause laughter when the wrong impressions they initially cause are rectified. For example, Cornelia wonders why life is so complicated. Frank has an immediate answer: 'Wir haben zu früh geheiratet.' (1) [We got married too early]. Cornelia is reminded that her husband used to say that as well. The audience will laugh, thinking that here is a married woman in bed with another man, having an extra-marital affair. But then their expectation is crushed in the next line, when Frank gently reminds Cornelia that she is in fact talking about her ex-husband. Laughter again—relief: at least as far as she is concerned, she is doing nothing inappropriate. Cornelia goes on: 'Natürlich mein ex-Mann. Sagt das deine Ehemalige auch?' [Of course my ex-husband. Does your ex say the same thing?]. Laughter again: so he is a divorcee as well. Later on in the same scene we learn that Cornelia is a teacher and Flatow skilfully integrates providing that information with more details about Cornelia (she has got a Ph.D.) and the night Cornelia and Frank have just spent together: a teacher by profession, Cornelia was able to teach Frank several new things during the night, which happened two days after they met for the first time. The conversation also reveals that both live in a block of flats, Cornelia on the third floor, Frank on the forth. Cornelia comments: 'Das ist auch besser so. Du oben, ich unten.' (4) [It's better that way, you upstairs and me downstairs], which Frank rightly understands as fleeting reference to sexual positions.

Zweite Geige also starts with a couple in bed. In a variation on Jäger's waking up in *Der Mann, der sich nicht traut...*, Felix tries to remember who the lady next to him might be, but unlike Jäger, he cannot. Only the clothes spread around the room remind him that she is Eva Maria, another one of the dancers in the theatre's ballet company and he smiles (7). Just as the couples in *Der Mann, der sich nicht traut...* and *Mein Vater, der Junggeselle*, Felix and Eva Maria engage in small talk after they have both woken up and Flatow again uses this conversation to create laughter and provide additional information about the characters. Eva Maria is surprised how late in the day it is already, how long she has slept and adds, with a reference to her childhood: 'Als Kind war ich kaum ins Bett zu kriegen.'(10) [When I was a child it was hard to get me into bed] Felix intentionally misunderstands and relates this childhood memory to how easy it was for him to seduce her when he comments on that memory ambiguously: 'Das hat sich ja gegeben.' [That's changed then]. Eva Maria initially nods in consent, then has a comic double take when she finally understands the ambiguity in Felix's comment and counters this with a reproachful protestation that she is not normally that easy to seduce.

Felix has his routines of seduction and good-bye: now he wants to get rid of Eva Maria; she has gone into the bathroom to have a shower and Felix phones his friend to help him—an established routine: the friend will call again in ten minutes pretending to inform Felix of an important recording they have been asked to attend, at short notice. Towards the end of the play we find out about another one of Felix's routines of seduction. He advises Knut, a huge rower, whose light breakfast, to the housekeeper Frau Baumgärtner's surprise, consists of six to seven slices of bread and malt beer, as to how he might win back his fiancée, Silvi, after she has fallen in love with Felix. Hulk Knut cannot comprehend why a woman like Silvi has fallen in love with a wimp like Felix. Felix suggests Knut go to talk to Silvi. The precise words he tells Knut to say to Silvi are those that he uses himself in his own seductions. Knut tries out Felix's idea and it works: Silvi comes back to him. Felix is disappointed, of course, but Eva Maria comes back to him and comforts him.

In *Romeo mit grauen Schläfen*, Alfi's attempts at seducing the starlet Gisi (pet name for Gisela) are fraught with problems, unexpected for Alfi, who has some experience in seduction. The main reason for the difficulties is that Vicky has left her baby in its basket in the room. Gisi comments how sweet the baby's eyes and nose are. This causes laughter because Vicky had mentioned earlier that the baby has Alfi's eyes and nose. Alfi is visibly proud and rubs his own nose on cue. Gisi drinks, but is worried that she will have the hiccups when she drinks sparkling wine or champagne and appropriately she has hiccups the very moment that Alfi tries to kiss her. After the hiccup has subsided, Alfi has another go at seducing her, using the standard phrases he has developed for this situation, similar to Felix in *Zweite Geige*:

> Alfi: Ach Gisi. Ich habs ja gleich gespürt.
> Gisi: Was?
> Alfi: Das wir zusammen gehören. Als du heute in die Kantine kamst, es war wie ein elektrischer Schlag. Ich wußte sofort, da kommt die Frau, auf die ich gewartet habe, ein ganzes Leben lang. (33)
> [Alfi: Oh Gisi. I felt it immediately.
> Gisi: What?
> Alfi: That we belong together. It was like an electric shock when you came into the canteen today. I knew immediately that here comes the woman I have been waiting for my whole life.]

The atmosphere Alfi has so cleverly created is broken by the baby's laughter at this very moment and again on cue a little later in the scene:

> Gisi: Ja?
> Alfi: Du, das ist ein schönes Gefühl.
> Gisi: Hast du das schon oft gehabt?

> Alfi: Wie kommst du denn darauf? Sowas hat man nur ein bis zweimal im Leben.
> (Das Baby lacht wieder. Alfi blickt vorwurfsvoll zur Tragetasche und schüttelt den Kopf) (33)
> [Gisi: Really?
> Alfi: You know that is a wonderful feeling....
> Gisi: Have you had it often?
> Alfi: What gave you that idea? Something like this only happens once or twice in a lifetime.
> (The baby laughs again. Alfi looks reproachfully at the basket and shakes his head)]

Innocent and naïve Gisi does not notice that the baby's response is ironic, commenting, as it were, on the false pretence that this declaration of love is Alfi's first. A little later in the scene, Gisi leaves for the theatre. She wants Alfi to pick her up immediately after the show. She wants to spend the night at his place and she says good-bye to 'Alfi-mouse.' After she has left, Alfi talks to the baby. He is shocked at Gisi's speed:

> Alfi: Alfimaus?! Die holen wir auch nicht ab. Will gleich hier übernachten, was denkt die sich eigentlich? Das wollen wir nicht.
> (Das Baby lacht. Alfi muß schmunzeln.)
> Alfi: Na ja. Wollen tun wir schon, aber nicht wenn wir sollen... (35)
> [Alfi: Alfimouse?! We are not going to pick her up. She wants to stay the night straight away. What is she thinking of? We don't want that.
>   (The baby laughs, Alfi has to smile to himself)
> Alfi: Well we want to, but not when we have to.]

In the same play, Jutta Hoffmann visits Alfi: she wants him to play the lead character in a television series based on a novel she has written. She makes a good impression on Alfi. They even talk about the fact that he once played Romeo. Flatow guides the conversation in such a way that the audience is guessing that she is the beloved from the past, but Alfi does not. Later in the play Jutta comes back and finally Alfi recognises her as the Julia he used to know a long time ago. He also discovers that he is the main character of her novel. They have to overcome a slight obstacle to their happiness, another misunderstanding: the young man Gisi has seen with Jutta is not her lover, as Gisi suspects, but her son. It becomes obvious to the audience at this stage that Alfi has the habit of passing his starlets on to his friend and manager Hayo and that Hayo's current mistress, a make-up artist, was probably also Alfi's lover before.

While Felix (*Zweite Geige*) and Alfi (*Romeo mit grauen Schläfen*) are experienced seducers, Ernst in *Verlängertes Wochenende* is most certainly not. In this play the audience is not led to laugh at attempts at getting rid of the girl after successful seduction, nor at seduction misfiring, but at seduction happening by coincidence, at least almost: Ernst sits down in a chair where Karin has earlier spilled the dressing of beef salad. He has to take off his trousers and she puts stain remover on them. He wears her dressing gown. Karin is sad, because Ricardo, whom she had invited for the weekend, had to be taken to hospital with a bad back after stepping on the keys Ernst returned and slipping and falling. She drinks more and more champagne and gets more and more drunk. Ernst is still with her. Crying, Karin leans against his arms. Eventually Karin asks Ernst to take her to bed, which he does. He has to carry her because she is so drunk that she cannot stand up or walk. The next morning Karin is surprised that Ernst is still there. She cannot remember anything. This results in several comical situations, when he tries to explain to her what did and what did not happen.

Flatow does not show the happy couple only in bed, but also in other day-to-day situations that provide equally rich material for comedy: in *Verlängertes Wochenende*, Karin and Ernst are having breakfast together and he is preparing rolls with liver sausage. Just as Karin is about to take her first bite of the roll, Ernst comments in passing that it's all the dog. Karin misunderstands, assuming she is about to eat dog meat. Ernst explains that he gets this wonderful liver sausage from the local butcher free of charge because the butcher is so grateful to Ernst for having saved his dog (62-3).

Couples are not always happy in their communication with each other: boulevard comedies derive equally humorous entertainment from their quarrels. In *Mein Vater, der Junggeselle,* Barbara tries to annoy ex-husband Frank by bringing a piano and a drum kit for son Thomas's use to Frank's new flat, in addition to a dagger, which also belongs to Thomas. Frank comments that now he is better able to understand why the criminal in the court case he attended that morning stabbed his wife: she bullied him, just as Barbara bullies Frank by bringing all those things into his flat (53). In the same play, Herr Schlüter, Barbara's new husband-to-be, who never appears on stage in person, is waiting downstairs in a red convertible, which he wants to give Thomas as a present for his eighteenth birthday. Thomas comes upstairs, is fairly annoyed, walks into his room and slams the door shut. Soon after that the phone rings. Frank answers it and hears from Herr Schlüter that Thomas was very rude to him when he gave him the convertible as a present:

> Frank: Was hat der Junge zu Ihnen gesagt? Sie sollen sich das Golf Cabriolet...Wohin sollen Sie sich das stecken? ...Nein, das ist wirklich unmöglich, schon rein technisch. Herr Schlüter, das ist mir natürlich sehr unangenehm, ich meine als Vater... (59)
> [What did the boy say to you? You should stick the convertible...where should you stick it? ... No, that's really impossible...I mean, just technically, to start with. Mr. Schlüter, I am very embarrassed by this, you know, as his father...]

The relationship between partners, both those who are already together and those who are—perhaps—about to pair up, sometimes without knowing or desiring, are central to boulevard comedy. The title of Florian Battermann's *Drum prüfe ewig, wer sich bindet*, which had its world premiere on 12 September 2003 at the Neues Theater, Hannover, directed by that theatre's artistic manager, James von Berlepsch, is a pun on a well-known saying in German, 'drum prüfe, wer sich ewig bindet': those who want to bind themselves forever in marriage should check each other out first. Battermann changes this to imply that those who want to bind themselves in marriage should check each other out forever. Bettina is about to get married when she suffers a minor accident at home, faints and wakes up to find that she can foresee the future with her husband-to-be and the man she almost chose instead of him. Battermann does not reveal to the audience which of the two men, gentle civil servant Bastian, or dashing pilot Mark was her intended husband-to-be. Bastian works with the municipal council's public gardening services office. In a number of scenes the audience sees what Bettina's future with him would be like: she embarks on a career, they have children and the end is not very happy for either of them. With Mark, her future is not much better, even if it is different. He is very successful in his career and can spend great amounts of money on Bettina, but he is impotent, or at least infertile for a number of years and the relationship as Bettina perceives it during her dream is not happy either. Once she wakes up, she decides not to get married at all. Instead she will move to Mallorca with her mother to get herself a rich pensioner.

Horst Pillau's *Buddha spricht nur mit Männern* (Buddha Talks to Men Only) provides an additional twist to the relationship motif: thanks to a Buddha statue and some meditation techniques, married couple Ulrich and Karin Burger manage to exchange their identities for one day: Ulrich's mind slips into Karin's body and he experiences her life and vice versa. Karin is surprised at the suppressed existence Ulrich leads in his job and decides to change things; she is also not pleased with his secretary's attempts at seduction. Ulrich, in turn, has some moments of despair while doing the household chores and experiences how silly men can be in their attempts at seduction when Karin gets her regular visit from her tutor of French and he courts her.

Elements of Farce

A good deal of the repertory of boulevard comedy theatres in Germany is made up of conventional farce, ranging from the French masters of the genre, Labiche and Feydeau, to British Ben Travers and Ray Cooney and some of Ayckbourn's earlier plays. At the centre of such plays are the extraordinary and increasing problems that suddenly emerge in the professional, domestic and private lives of ordinary people. The problems are in most cases caused by others, enveloping the main characters of farce in increasingly complicated situations that they are less and less in control of, despite increased and frantic efforts. The situation ends in chaos and leaves the main characters in a state of despair, questioning their previously well-defined identities. Characters tend to be stereotypes, important because of their functions in the plays and not necessarily because of their psychological depth. They can appear one-dimensional and superficial. Dramatists of farce use their characters' verbal language predominantly to create misunderstandings. In such cases, the characters will use all kinds of non-verbal language to compensate, but equally without success. Time is important in farce: characters are under pressure of time, adding to their despair and to their desperate and futile attempts to try to avoid further disaster; for the actors, precise timing is one of the most essential abilities needed to create laughter. Elements of the set and props take on an equally important role in the mechanism of farce, with doors, tables, beds, balconies and curtains offering repeated opportunities for characters to hide themselves or others or unwanted objects (Drechsler, 1988: 26-35).

Ray Cooney is probably the most well respected writer of farce in Britain today. He trained on the job as an actor in repertory and soon started writing farces. One of Ray Cooney's first professional appearances as an actor was in *Dry Rot* by John Chapman, whom he claims among his mentors. Later, he co-wrote *Not Now Darling*, *There goes the Bride*, *Move over Mrs. Markham* and *My Giddy Aunt* with Chapman. Cooney's *Run for your Wife* became his greatest early success in 1982, followed, in 2001 with an at least equally successful sequel, *Caught in the Act*. Both plays centre around South London taxi driver John Smith, who is a cheerful bigamist, married both to Barbara in Streatham and to Mary in nearby Wimbledon. His flexible working hours as a taxi driver allow him to arrange his time to accommodate his double life. In *Run for your Wife*, his precision timing is threatened when he is admitted to the hospital after an accident; his wives inform two different police stations; two police inspectors take up their investigations. Smith is returned from hospital to one of his wives at the wrong time and his friend and neighbour Stanley bears the comical brunt of helping him save his skin. At the end, Smith continues his bigamous life. At the beginning of *Caught in the Act*, time has moved on eighteen years. Smith's two children from his two wives, Vicky (with Mary) and Gavin (with Barbara), have met through an internet chatroom and want to go on their first date. Of course, John has to prevent this meeting from happening and again Stanley has to help. At the end of the play, a desperate John confesses to his wives, expecting a double divorce. However, they have known for some sixteen years and are actually happy with the arrangement: they don't have to do the full load of housework and they get frequent surprises and new developments in their sex lives. The children, too, may continue their romance, because one of them is not really John's—Stanley has made a lasting mark on the family in more than the obvious way as a tenant.

Flatow's plays are not pure farces. His characters have more depth than those in farce, they are not mere cogs in the mechanism of farce. Flatow's plots themselves are not, as in farce, mechanical. However, he employs elements of farce in his plays, for example, unexpected events of various kinds. There is the unexpected and uninvited visitor. After having spent their first night together, Frank and Cornelia in *Mein Vater, der Junggseselle* get up, start dressing and prepare breakfast. Then the doorbell rings. Frank is startled: visitors this early in the morning are not welcome, especially since he has a female visitor.

>Frank: Ich komme ja schon. Wer ist da?
>Thomas: *(von draußen)* Ich Papi.
>Frank: *(überrascht)* Wer?
>Thomas: *(von draußen)* Dein Sohn.
>Frank: Tommi?
>Thomas: *(von draußen)* Wer sonst? Ich denke ich bin ein Einzelkind?
>Frank: *(nervös)* Wie? Ja natürlich.
>Thomas: *(von draußen)* Willst du mich nicht reinlassen? (12)
>[Frank: I'm coming, who is it?
>Thomas: *(from outside)* It's me daddy
>Frank: *(surprised)* Who?

Thomas: *(from outside)* Your son.
Frank: Tommi?
Thomas: *(from outside)* Who else? I thought I was an only child.
Frank: *(nervous)* What? Yes, of course.
Thomas: *(from outside)* Don't you want to let me in?]

Frank has to act quickly and tries to persuade Cornelia to leave, as gently and diplomatically as possible.

Frank: Tust du mir einen großen Gefallen?
Cornelia: Ich soll verschwinden.
Frank: Nein. Ich will dich doch nicht wegschicken. Doch nur ....wenn er dich hier sieht. Was soll er dann von mir denken.
Cornelia: Ach darfst du sowas noch nicht?
Frank: Nein....Ich meine doch. Aber...Ich habe ihm doch noch nichts von dir erzählt. (12)
    [Frank: Will you do me a big favour?
Cornelia: You want me to disappear?
Frank: No. I don't want to send you away. But....if he sees you here, what will he think of me?
Cornelia: Aren't you allowed yet to do something like this?
Frank: No...I mean of course. But I haven't told him about you yet.]

The unexpected visitor features also in *Romeo mit grauen Schläfen*. Alfi is waiting for a visit from a starlet, yet another one. But his daughter Vicky turns up instead and is initially mistaken by Frau Bethge, the housekeeper, to be the new girlfriend. Vicky brings a large basket, in which she carries a baby. Vicky asks, when she notices that Frau Bethge is looking at her thoughtfully:

Ist was?
Frau Bethge: Nein, nein. Ich bin nur überrascht. Ich kann mir nicht vorstellen daß Herr Fischer ein Kind erwartet.
Vicky: *(ironisch)* Ich mir auch nicht. Im allgemeinen werden nur Frauen schwanger. (14)
Vicky: What's the matter?
Frau Bethge: Nothing, nothing. I am only surprised. I can't imagine that Mr Fischer is expecting a baby.
Vicky: *(ironically)* I can't imagine that either, usually only women become pregnant.]

When Alfi enters, he is dressed very smartly, all the seducer, but without his glasses. He therefore does not recognise his daughter. When the expected visitor arrives Frau Bethge opens the door, dryly commenting: 'Noch eine.' (23) [And here's another one.]

In *Verlängertes Wochenende*, there are two unexpected visitors. Karin wants to have a shower before her date for the weekend, Ricardo, arrives. As she enters the bathroom she screams, walks out, searches for the phone, tries to call the police but does not remember the emergency phone number. Ernst, the unexpected visitor, who is already in the flat and has just been taking a shower himself, to prepare for his weekend with Doris, appears in the bathroom door. He is dripping wet and has temporarily wrapped a towel around his waist, which he has to hold on to with both hands. Karin finds out that Doris invited Ernst for the wrong weekend. The zip of Karin's dress is wide open at the back and every time she turns her back to Ernst he modestly closes his eyes, which she notices, of course, once she faces him again. Eventually she gets irritated enough by it to ask him what's wrong with his eyes.

The scene contains farcical elements of slapstick. For example, Ernst tries to hold his towel in place with his elbows and at the same time tries to close her zip. While doing so his hair gets caught in the zip and he has to work much harder at it than before. At one point he is looking in his pockets for his own house keys, which he naturally cannot find in the towel. When Ernst wants to leave, he surprises Ricardo and Karin flirting. He wants to retreat quickly, falls over his travelling bag, which is in the way, crashing to the floor along with the suitcase he is carrying.

Ernst tries to leave several times, but repeatedly fails. First he forgets his trousers, then he leaves behind his keys to the block of flats; when the doorbell rings for the third time, Ricardo and Karin are exasperated:

> Ricardo: Jetzt hat es aber geklingelt.
> Karin: Laß ihn doch, die Wohnungstür ist doch abgeschlossen.
> Ricardo: *(grimmig)* Der kommt durchs Schlüsselloch. (34)
> [Ricardo: That was the doorbell.
> Karin: Ignore him, the door of the flat is locked.
> Ricardo: *(grumpy)* That one gets in though the keyhole.]

Another common characteristic of farce is misunderstanding. At some point in the course of *Mein Vater, der Junggseselle*, Frank sleeps with his ex-wife, Barbara. No other character in the play knows about this. On the day they all celebrate Tommy's graduating from high school, Barbara arrives and it is abundantly clear she is pregnant. She says that she is due in two to three weeks, which would mean that the baby was conceived when she slept with Frank. This causes humorous situations. For example, Barbara tells Frank how happy Georg, her new partner, is about having a baby:

> Barbara: Georg hatte Tränen in den Augen, als er das sah, nämlich das Bild von dem scan. Überhaupt das wir ein Kind bekommen, er ist so dankbar.
> Frank: Wem?
> Barbara: Dem Schicksal. Wem sonst? (96-7)
> [Barbara: Georg had tears in his eyes when he saw it, the picture of the scan, that is. Anyway, that we are having a baby, he is so grateful.
> Frank: To whom?
> Barbara: To whom? To fate, what else?]

Frank obviously believes that he is the baby's father and the following conversation with Cornelia adds to his distress:

> Cornelia: Du ich finde deine ex Frau hat sich sehr verändert. Sie ist so lieb geworden.
> Frank: Findest du?
> Cornelia: Na ja wenn man Mutter wird, ein schönes Gefühl.
> Frank: Sag bloß du beneidest Sie?
> Cornelia: Jetzt nicht mehr.
> Frank: *(stirnrunzelnd)* Jetzt nicht mehr?
> Cornelia *(schüttelt den Kopf)* Seitdem ich weiß, daß du Vater wirst.
> Frank *(stottert)* Du..Du..Du weißt das?
> Cornelia: Ich weiß es genau.
> Frank: Seit wann?
> Cornelia: Seit gestern.
> Frank: Seit gestern? Von wem?
> Cornelia: Von meinem Arzt.
> Frank: Was denn, du bekommst auch ein Kind von mir?...Ich meine Du bekommst auch ein Kind?
> Cornelia: *(nickt)* Du wirst dich aber noch ein wenig gedulden müssen. Ich bin erst im zweiten Monat. (99)
> [Cornelia: I find that your ex wife has changed a lot. She has become really lovely.
> Frank: You think so?
> Cornelia: Well, when you become a mother, it is a nice feeling.
> Frank: Are you saying that you envy her?
> Cornelia: Not anymore.
> Frank: *(frowns)* Not anymore?
> Cornelia: *(shakes her head)* Since I know that you are going to be a dad.

> Frank: *(stutters)* You, you, you know?
> Cornelia: I know it precisely.
> Frank: Since when?
> Cornelia: Since yesterday.
> Frank: Since yesterday? From whom?
> Cornelia: From my doctor.
> Frank: What? You are also having a baby by me? ... I mean, you are having a baby, too?
> Cornelia: *(nods)* But you'll have to be patient. I am only two months along.]

Thomas explains to Frank that he had moved in with him in order to unite his parents again.

> Thomas: Und es hat ja geklappt, oder etwa nicht? Durch mich bist Du doch wieder mit Mutti in Berührung gekommen.
> Frank: *(nach einer kleinen Pause)* Du sagst es. (103)
> [Thomas: And it worked didn't it? Because of me you came back into contact with mum.
> Frank: *(after a short pause)* You said it.]

Farcically mistaken identities are also cause for much laughter in *Verlängertes Wochenende*: Ricardo cannot stay the night with Karin, as planned, because he slipped, fell and had to be taken to hospital with a bad back. When Ricardo returns the next day he sees Doris. They both like each other. When a little later he meets Ernst, he thinks that Ernst has spent the night with Doris and does not mind. On the other hand Ernst does not know that Doris is there and he thinks that Ricardo does not mind that he obviously spend the night with Karin. Originally Ricardo wanted to spend the night with her. Ricardo is comfortable with Ernst now and they eat caviar together and drink sparkling wine that Ricardo brought with him. Then Doris comes into the picture. She thinks that Karin has slept with Ernst. Finally a young and well-dressed woman appears, asking to speak to her husband. Who could that be, Ernst or Ricardo? The audience is left with this question at the end of the scene before the interval. In the next scene, after a long to and fro it is established that the woman isn't Ernst's wife, but Ricardo's.

If laughter is directed at something (an object) or someone (a subject), it creates distance; it isolates the object or subject at which laughter is directed from the one who laughs. In contrast, laughter with a subject or object creates integration of the laughing person, the laughing spectator and the subject or object of laughter (Turk, 1993). Writers of boulevard comedy insist that one of the most important aspects of their genre is to write characters that are credible and believable, characters, that is, with whom an audience can easily identify. Such characters provide the starting point for farce, but there, as one of its current major representatives, Ray Cooney, argues, the writer necessarily manipulates the characters to fit the patterns of farce, leading from an outwardly ordinary situation into more and more outrageous complications that cause more and more laughter (2003). The main characters, under pressure from the dilemma they face, seek to save themselves with all kinds of inventions, lies and tricks, only to find, towards the end, that they have forgotten, in the chaos they have created, the intricate storylines they have produced. The nature of farce leads implicitly to more instances of laughter at, rather than laughter with, a character.

None of Flatow's characters is ideal, they all have their weaknesses, their strange habits and idiosyncrasies. However, they all remain essentially likeable throughout. One major device for creating such an affinity between audience and character is that Flatow regularly provides background information on each major character, thus allowing the audience to become familiar with him or her. While pure farce may lead to a predominance of laughing at characters, in Flatow's plays there is certainly more laughing with characters, leading to identification of spectator with characters.

Flatow uses special devices, challenges to the props department, to farcical effect in *Verlängertes Wochenende* and *Romeo mit grauen Schläfen*. In the latter play, Vicky's baby laughs or cries according to the necessity of the situation. Flatow insists, in the stage directions, that the laughing or crying must come from the baby basket. When Frau Bethge comes and looks into the basket, the baby starts crying and as soon as she leaves, the baby stops (19). A little later in the play, Alfi has a talk with Vicky and the baby comments at appropriate places:

> Alfi: Ich habe weiß Gott nichts gegen uneheliche Kinder, aber sie müssen ja nicht unbedingt unsere Familie beglücken.
> *(Das Kind schreit)*
> Alfi: *(In Richtung Tasche.)* Entschuldige, ich habe es ja nicht so gemeint. Der Junge ist aber sehr empfindlich.
> Vicky: Wie du.
> *(Baby beruhigt sich)* (23)
> [Alfi: God knows I really have nothing against illegitimate children, but they mustn't necessarily favor our family with their presence.
> *(Baby screams)*
> Alfi: *(towards baby carrier)* Sorry, I didn't mean it. That boy is very sensitive.
> Vicky: Just like you.

(Baby calms down)]

Hayo is Alfi's friend and manager. He talks about Vera, Alfi's ex-wife:

> Hayo: Deine Vera ist eine Frau die man sein ganzes Leben lang sucht.
> Alfi: Bis man sie hat. (41)
> [Hayo: Your Vera, she is a woman one looks for all one's life...
> Alfi: Until you have got her.]

The baby laughs at this comment. Not at all expecting a baby to be in the room, Hayo at first mistakes the baby's laugh for Alfi's, then produces a double-take. After Flatow has introduced this technical device and created much laughter with it, he finally breaks the expectations that he will create another laugh: Alfi tells Vicky about the one great love of his life. He explains that the girl he had fallen in love with was too young then, not yet sixteen. He had promised her to wait for her. However, this did not work out:

> Alfi: Drei Wochen später habe ich deine liebe Mutter kennengelernt. Sie hat mir viel im Leben kaputt gemacht. (49)
> [Alfi: I met your dear mother three weeks later. She has destroyed a lot of things in my life.]

The baby starts crying at this cue. Alfi follows viewers' expectations in interpreting the crying:

> Alfi: Es fühlt mit mir. (49)
> [Alfi: He knows my feelings.]

But Vicky breaks his and the audience's expectations, causing laughter:

> Vicky: Nein. Er hat Hunger. Ist ja auch schon zehn Minuten über die Zeit. (49)
> [Vicky: No, he is hungry. It's ten minutes past the time.]

In *Verlängertes Wochenende*, Ernst forgets Max, his turtle, which according to Flatow's stage directions, has to be remote-controlled.

> Ernst: Ich war vorhin so in Eile und da habe ich Max vergessen.
> Karin: Max?
> Ricardo: Wer ist denn noch alles in der Wohnung?
> Karin: Weiß ich doch nicht.
> Ricardo: Man stolpert ja förmlich über Männer.

Ernst: (lässt sich auf die Knie nieder und beginnt unter den Möbeln zu suchen) Das wollte ich ja gerade vermeiden. Er ist ja ziehmlich klein.
Ricardo: Der Herr ist wohl Lilliputaner?
Ernst: Max ist kein Herr sondern eine Dame. Eigentlich mehr ein Mädchen, aber das wußten die Vorbesitzer nicht und nun hört sie auf Max.
(Er findet ein Paar von Ricardos Hemdknöpfen und reicht sie ihm)
Ernst: Die gehören wohl Ihnen.
(guckt unter den Plattenspieler)
Ernst: Da bist du ja, natürlich. Hätte ich mir ja auch denken können. Max ist sehr musikalisch.
(Er holt eine Schildkröte hervor) (25)
[Ernst: I was in such a hurry earlier that I forgot Max.
        Karin: Max?
Ricardo: Who else is in the flat then?
Karin: I really don't know.
Ricardo: One is literally falling over men in this place.
Ernst: *(gets down on his knees and starts looking under the furniture)* This is what I wanted to avoid, as he's quite small.
Ricardo: Might the gentleman be a dwarf?
Ernst: Max isn't a gentleman, but a lady. Actually more a girl, but the previous owners didn't know this and now she answers to the name of Max. (He finds several of Ricardo's shirt buttons and hands them to him) Presumably these belong to you?
(Looks under the record player)
Ernst: There you are, of course. I should have thought of that. Max is very musical. *(He retrieves a turtle)*]

Later in the play further reference to the turtle creates more laughter, when Ernst recalls that he had turtle soup recently and Max went into sulky hiding for two days.

To summarise: the repertory of boulevard comedy theatres in Germany consists of plays predominantly from the United States of America, the United Kingdom and France in German translation and plays written in German by dramatists specializing in boulevard comedy theatre, such as Flatow, Pillau and Vögel. These plays share a range of typical characteristics regarding the set, the use of telephone conversations, the reliance on efficient scene endings, the exploitation of professional clichés and variations of the generation gap and couples as central characters, all to derive situations and dialogue that allows the audience to laugh. While some percentage of the repertory is farce, most other plays in the repertory contain at least elements of farce.

Notes

1 'Schöner wohnen' is the name of an annual exhibition and a monthly magazine in Germany advertising new design for making the home more beautiful.

2 Curth Flatow, *Zweite Geige*, 5. As with most boulevard comedies in Germany, the texts are not published in book form available to the general public, but merely as typescripts. Theaters wishing to produce any such play have to apply to the company that holds the manuscript on behalf of the author and also serves as the author's agent. That company will issue a contract setting the royalties payable by the theatre and will, at the same time, send a sufficient number of copies of the script in question for production purposes. In some cases, those scripts must be returned after the production's run is over. *Zweite Geige* is handled by Felix Bloch Erben, Berlin.

3 The association between the medicine and someone's age has potential for being humourous because of the popularity from television and radio advertisement, in Germany, of over the counter medicines and health food drinks and tablets intended to enhance the quality of life in old age. Where such popularity does not exist, spectators are not likely to make the association and the potential for humour is lost.

4 This is a main characteristic also of Flatow's *Vater einer Tochter* (Father of a Daugher, 1966). Berlin: Felix Bloch Erben.

CHAPTER THREE

ASPECTS OF TRANSLATION

Many of the plays on the stages of boulevard comedy theatres in Germany are presented in German translation from an original in a different language, in the hope, or under the assumption that audiences in Germany will laugh as much about elements considered humorous in their source context (i.e., predominantly in the United Kingdom, in the United States of America, or in France) as people in those countries. Such an assumption involves two different lines of argument and thus analysis: aspects of cultural context and aspects of language.

Cultural contexts

If laughter were considered solely culture-specific and not culture-independent or universal, audiences in one cultural context might not understand and thus not laugh about the jokes dominant in a different culture. Evidence from German boulevard comedy theatres, however, suggests that at least some elements of laughter are shared across cultures: otherwise the plays from cultures outside Germany would not succeed to the extent they do.

It is equally evident, however, where the transfer of laughter across cultures reaches its limits. The German reception of Alan Ayckbourn's plays is a case in point. Artistic managers of boulevard comedy theatres in Germany would place a play by Flatow or Cooney into their repertories without much thought, because their plays are known as audience magnets and thus guarantee commercial success. However, they would be rather cautious with an Ayckbourn play, giving their decision to include it much thought.[1] Martin Woelffer, of Berlin's boulevard comedy theatres, explains that 'Germans tend to lack the ability to laugh about themselves,' (2001) which he considers to be a major requirement for appreciating Ayckbourn's humour. He confirms that Ayckbourn's own productions cause much laughter with a light touch, whereas in Germany Ayckbourn's comedy easily mutates into heavy Chekhovian material. A good example of this is the televised production of Ayckbourn's *Season's Greetings*, directed by one of Germany's leading stage directors Andrea Breth (b. 1952). The original production in the United Kingdom, directed by Ayckbourn himself, lasted approximately two and a half hours including interval. The audience's laughter was abundant. Breth's production lasted about four hours and offered hardly any opportunity for laughter: Breth directed Ayckbourn as a contemporary Chekhov tragedy—at the time Breth was most renowned for her Chekhov productions. Christa Bode, wife and personal assistant to Elert Bode, who was artistic manager of the Komödie im Marquardt, Stuttgart, from 1976 to 2002, also argues that Ayckbourn is problematic for boulevard comedy theatres in general because the typically British humour is not to everyone's taste and particularly so in the Stuttgart region. American humour, in her view, is a different matter: German audiences had been conditioned to American culture to a larger extent through television series such as *Dallas* (2001).

If the boulevard comedy theatres' artistic managers decide to include Ayckbourn in their repertories, they do so, typically, in an attempt of attracting new audiences to their theatres—perhaps from the municipal theatres where audiences are more used to Ayckbourn. The Wölffer management in Berlin explicitly sought to attract new star actors to their theatres as audience magnets (Woelffer, 2001). To be able to persuade some stars from serious theatre or film into boulevard theatre, the Wölffers tend to offer them roles to play by, among others, Ayckbourn. Thus, in 2001, actor and director Uwe Eric Laufenberg and film star Katja Riemann appeared in Ayckbourn's *Intimate Exchanges*, with Laufenberg also directing. The unusual feature of the play is that Riemann plays all the female parts and Laufenberg all the male parts. The various male and female characters are extremely different and the change of costume and appearance, of body posture and idiosyncrasies alone, from one character to the next, was enough to cause gales of laughter in the United Kingdom. In Berlin, Laufenberg and Riemann managed the changes without technical difficulty, but hardly such that they caused much laughter in comparison with the production in the United Kingdom. The national press, represented by the *Frankfurter Allgemeine Zeitung* and *Die Welt*, which otherwise tends to ignore boulevard comedy productions, sent its reviewers. They were not impressed: Katja Riemann's acting was criticised as lacking nuances and depth (Anon., 2001), and as not capable of raising any feelings of compassion or sympathy with her characters, which the *Welt* critic harshly attributed to Riemann's touchy personality (Krause, 2001). The critics' views confirm and thus validate my own critical impression that neither Riemann nor Laufenberg took their characters seriously enough. This showed particularly in the uneasy shifts between solid characterization and intentional, conscious and thus noticeable dropping of punch lines. Awkward pauses resulted at times when such punch lines were delivered with blatant mistiming or the wrong intonation and the audience did not laugh.

When the boulevard comedy theatres in Germany experiment with Ayckbourn, they thus clearly risk failure—but if their gamble pays off, they can attract and keep new stars and new audiences. The theatres do not face the risk potentially caused by cultural differences with the majority of plays written in the native language of the audiences, German. For example, a popular choice for the repertories is a series of sketches by Loriot. In 'Das Bild hängt schief' (The Picture's Not Straight), Loriot plays a fastidious vacuum cleaner salesman. He is in the middle of demonstrating his machines, which is already hilarious because of the incredibly complex terminology he uses in his explanations of the vacuum cleaner's advantages, when the homemaker has to leave him to attend to her cooking in the kitchen. Loriot looks around the nice and tidy living room and notices that one picture frame on one of the walls is not straight. He decides to do something about it and gets up to straighten it. What follows is a nightmare of disaster, as, in an intricate domino effect, he accidentally pushes over a vase, which pushes over the next thing and when he tries to remedy this, the next item crashes down and so on. A little later, when the homemaker cheerfully returns from her cooking, the room looks as if it has been ransacked by burglars. Loriot is also completely dishevelled and apologetically explains: 'The picture wasn't straight.' In the second example, Loriot plays a middle-aged, very formal and shyly inhibited man who meets a lady for the first time whom he has contacted through a lonely-hearts column in an up-market newspaper. They are in a restaurant, eating the starter, soup. The soup has spaghetti in it and a short piece of spaghetti ends up on Loriot's cheek. The lady is surprised, which Loriot attributes to some banal remark he has just made, so he takes pains to explain the remark even more clearly. The piece of spaghetti meanwhile travels from Loriot's cheek to his nose, to his chin, to his other cheek, to his forehead and so on, while the lady gets more and more frustrated and disgusted. Loriot in turn gets more and more frantic in his attempts to appease the lady, increasingly insecure and not at all aware why she reacts in this way to him. The waiter comes, notices the piece of spaghetti on Loriot's face, is also disgusted, takes away the soup and brings the main course. Finally the piece of spaghetti falls from Loriot's face on-to the plate. Loriot sees it after it has fallen, is himself disgusted and summons the waiter, complaining that there is a piece of spaghetti on the plate. Assuming audiences in Germany have seen some of Loriot's work before, they will compare in their minds the performance by the respective theatre's production with their memory of those sketches on television. If they missed a particular sketch in its original, they would at least be able to imagine what it would have been like with Loriot himself and Evelyn Hamann. Such knowledge adds to the enjoyment of the sketches.

Gottfried Greiffenhagen and Frank Wittenbrink's revue *Veronika, der Lenz ist da* has been one of the most popular productions at boulevard comedy theatres since its premiere in 1997 in Berlin, directed by Martin Woelffer. It is a biographical play about the members of the *Comedian Harmonists*, a band of six men—five vocalists and a pianist, who rose to fame in 1928 but were forced out of existence as a result of Nazi politics by 1934. Since its phenomenal success in 1997, the actors recruited by the Berlin boulevard comedy theatres for the production of a play initially scheduled to run for the usual two to three months, have repeatedly got back together for revivals of the play, both in Berlin and on tour. They formed the *Berlin Comedian Harmonists* and have been similarly successful on a number of tours across Germany with a repertory of songs from the original Comedian Harmonists. The group's and the production's success, are due to the feelings of nostalgia they stir in the audience. Nostalgia is equally essential to the successes of a revue like *Hossa*, put on by Komödie Fürth and featuring German pop songs of the 1970s and two plays at Komödie Kassel, which showed members of the Wöhlermann family in the 1970s and 1980s, respectively. Klaus Chatten's *Klassentreffen*, directed in Berlin by Martin Woelffer in 2003, is about two middle aged men who meet again after many years and share reminiscences of their school days together in the 1970s.

Language

The majority of the plays on the stages of boulevard comedy theatres in Germany are translations of plays from the United Kingdom, United States of America or France. The commercial success of the boulevard comedy theatres' productions of the plays suggests two related things: for one, the kind of humour found in the plays is comprehensible across cultures and secondly, the translators play their part in making some humour accessible to their target (German) audiences by exercising an amount of poetic license in their translations. Reference to translations of Flatow's plays into English should serve to confirm this claim.

Some phrases that have the potential of causing laughter in one language simply cannot be translated accurately because the target language does not have any equivalent words needed to carry the material causing laughter. The original title of one of Flatow's plays is *Der Mann, der sich nicht traut...* On the surface, the translation is straightforward: *The Man Who Does Not Dare...* with the ellipsis at the end indicating whatever the play is likely to show as instances of him not daring. However, *trauen* has several further meanings, on its own and in its reflexive form, *sich trauen*. It is *to trust*. So the man who does not dare is also the man who does not trust, who does not trust himself, has no self-confidence. The three meanings fit the central character of this play well: Jäger is indeed not a daredevil, he does not trust others and he does not have much self-confidence, under a veneer of suave modishness. *Trauen* has a further meaning, though, related to the noun *Trauung*, which means wedding ceremony. Jäger is civil servant who conducts marriages, *er traut*. Of course he cannot and would not want to, if he could, conduct the ceremony at his own wedding. Flatow plays with all four meanings in one word, in relation to the character and the plot of the play. It is impossible to render all this in English or any other language, because there is no word to do this multiple pun justice. Flatow calls *Der Mann, der sich nicht traut...Ein Stück von Curth Flatow*. Again, superficially this line simply means: *A Play by Curth Flatow*, where *Stück* is given its non-literal meaning of stage or theatre play. The literal meaning of *Stück* is *piece* and Flatow intended the pun, presenting the material of the play—distrust regarding the institution of marriage—as a piece of himself, having gone through a divorce in his own life and remembering it well (Flatow, 2000: 174).

Another example, taken from Flatow's *Romeo mit grauen Schläfen*, is a line from the text itself (rather than a part of a play's title) that is impossible to translate in such as way as to keep its potential for creating laughter in the audience: actor Alfi comments on a middle-aged female colleague who has just undergone a face-lift. His manager Hayo says that she has changed quite a bit, to which Alfi replies: 'Verändert ist gut, die sah aus wie ein postalischer Begriff, unbekannt verzogen.' (106) Literally, this translates as: 'Changed is good, she looked like a term from the post office: moved to unknown destination.' The pun is on the word *verzogen*, which means *moved house*. It is the past participle of *verziehen*, to move house, but more literally it also means to distort, in the specific sense of applying tensions to a malleable substance so as to change its usual appearance in a way that is considered aesthetically displeasing. Thus what Alfi says here, using the pun on the post office jargon, is that the face of the actress in question has been distorted (*verzogen*) to such an extent that she is now unrecognisable (*unbekannt, not known*).

In other cases, a literal translation of a line does not do full justice to the original's humour, but a rendering in the idiom of the target language is more effective and keeps the meaning intended by the writer. In *Der Mann, der sich nicht traut...*, for example, Jäger is seen arguing with his son Ullrich. Jäger comments sarcastically on Ullrich's dull, dark clothes, ending with 'You could possibly wear a more colourful shirt.' Ullrich's brief, equally sarcastic, response, *Du kaum*, literally translates as *you hardly*. 'You hardly' sounds wooden and stilted: it works better in production to give Ullrich a different line, such as 'You'd have a job', which is short for 'It would take you a lot of effort, it would be a major job for you, to wear a more colourful shirt than the one you're wearing now', a reference to the stage directions at the beginning of the scene, which demand that Jäger is wearing a shirt that is outrageously colourful (12).

Jäger continues by saying that the shirt in question needs to go into the wash. Ullrich retorts: *In die Altkleidersammlung*. The literal translation is *Into the old clothes collection*. This is something German audiences can relate to: every now and then, the Red Cross, or a similar organization, distributes large plastic bags with their logo and the word 'Altkleidersammlung' on them and people are encouraged to put any discarded clothes into it and place the bag by the roadside on a particular day for pickup. Such a practice is unknown in the United Kingdom, for example, so here the line would need to be changed to *into the charity shop*, which is an approximate equivalent that United Kingdom audiences can relate to. Differences between British English (BE) and American English (AE) are of course also relevant for translation: depending on the target audience, in *Der Mann, der sich nicht traut...*, for example, Julia and Jäger encounter either a power cut (BE) or power outage (AE) and Jäger's profession, Standesbeamter, makes sense to a British audience as 'registrar' or 'registry officer', while in the United States of America matters are more difficult because here the legal ceremony of a wedding and the license, are dealt with by a lawyer or a justice of the peace (magistrate), who have a range of other duties. In contrast, the registrar's activities are limited to marriages and registering births and deaths and issuing certificates related to these.

To summarise: while there are isolated and well identified areas where cultural transfer of laughter faces difficulties, the practice and the success of boulevard comedy in Germany, with a repertory comprising many plays from the United States of America, the United Kingdom and France in translation into German, suggests that these cultures have enough in common to make the transfer of laughter possible.

Note

1 This view was voiced by Martin Woelffer (artistic manager, Berlin), Angelika Ober (artistic manager, Münster), Frank Bischoff (dramaturg, Kassel), Markus Exner (dramaturg, Frankfurt), Claus Helmer (artistic manager, Frankfurt) and Dieter Rummel (Darmstadt), in interviews with the author.

Chapter Four

Production and Reception of Boulevard Comedy

Acting in Boulevard Comedy

Actors in tragedy, or in serious realistic plays, are supported by the weight of both plot and message. A serious or tragic character offers much material for actors to show their impressive abilities and to attract audience attention and admiration. In boulevard comedy, the message tends to be lightweight. The plot in boulevard comedy is not complex, but predominantly functional, serving to manoeuvre the characters into situations the audiences can laugh at, or that the writer can use for dialogue that causes laughter. Characters in boulevard comedy are not as complex and thus rewarding for actors either, compared with characters in tragedy. Thus, since boulevard comedy has less to offer as far as a complex plot, a serious, gripping message and rich and rewarding material for the actors are concerned, it demands a range of more sophisticated technical skills from its actors: it is those skills that allow the actors to compensate for the lack of complexity and resulting richness characteristic of tragedy and serious realistic plays (Spier, 2004: 198-9).

Actors and directors specializing in boulevard comedy tend to agree that acting in this specific genre of theatre is different from acting at municipal or state theatres (Höckmann, 2001; Spier, 2001, 2003; Rummel, 2003; Helmer, 2003). In contrast, actors working predominantly at municipal or state theatres insist that the only difference is good or bad acting, which can apply to any genre and any venue—in other words, they deny that there is anything different, or special about acting at a boulevard comedy theatre (May, 2003; Alisch, 2003). Some of those actors deny that they consider colleagues who work mainly in boulevard theatres inferior, but at the same time they can easily lapse into comments such as: 'A colleague I went to acting school with made quite a good start at such and such a state theatre, but has now ended up in boulevard comedy.' (Alisch, 2003). Boulevard comedy demands of its actors a very thorough understanding of the characters they are playing. While this applies to any theatre production, actors in tragedy or serious plays might get away with less thorough understanding because the production is supported substantially by the plot and the message. In boulevard comedy, such support does not exist. As Höckmann puts it: 'In boulevard comedy, every character has to be understood as a very serious person, who has all the good and bad sides that people tend to have, who leads a normal life and is thrust into extraordinary circumstances of which they try to make the best they can, to survive (2001). Wolfgang Spier, the King of Boulevard, confirms that particularly when playing comedy, actors have to take their parts seriously (Spier, 2004: 199). To demonstrate this: Jäger, the title character in *Der Mann, der sich nicht traut*...is a man who has suffered a major blow when he found out his wife's infidelity and who has not recovered from that blow too well, really, because behind the façade of a self-assured, modern, energetic man lurks a miserable, unhappy and authoritarian alter-ego. The other characters in the play are similarly written as full-fledged characters, all with their good and bad sides. Julia is still unmarried despite her good looks and moves from one relationship with a married man to the next. Her niece, Gaby, comes across as sweet but shallow, an impression that the audience shares with her own fiancé, Ullrich, who does not hide is occasional exasperation. Fräulein Lamm allows herself to be exploited by Jäger in their once-a-week, no-commitment relationship. All those characters would fare well in a serious play: each of the features of their characters could be used, in a genre other than comedy, for very serious, moving and tragic plot structures and could carry profound messages.

The actors wishing to play those characters convincingly need to be aware of the characters' dark sides, to make them believable to the audience. Only if actors take their characters seriously do they have a chance of causing laughter in the audience. Actors who try to be funny are bound to fail. With the understanding of their characters as the basis, actors in boulevard comedy need to be aware acutely that they are playing comedy and that awareness needs to be expressed in a certain edge to their acting, both physical and in the way they speak, the way they present the punch lines. In contrast to realistic acting, typically appropriate for playing characters in a play by Ibsen, such as *A Doll's House* or *Hedda Gabler*, in boulevard comedy emphases in spoken dialogue are differently placed. The words or word that contain the trigger for laughter can be preceded by a pause or a piece of business. The trigger is usually placed at the end of a sentence. The actor, therefore, has to place special emphasis on those last words of the sentence and articulate them particularly well and clearly. The body should support the words: the actor might decide to move, if appropriate, on a line preceding the punchline, but not to move on the punch line so as to avoid visual distraction from it (Sievers, Stiver, Kahan, 1974: 191).

Actors are not on stage alone and can support each other in their aim of making the audience laugh. Usually in boulevard comedy, a few straight lines lead up to a punch line, which usually contains an element of the unexpected. The lead-ups should be delivered clearly and seriously and when one actor reaches a punch line, the others on stage should avoid moving, gesturing or reacting (Sievers, Stiver, Kahan, 1974: 191). Once the audience starts laughing, the actors with the next line must time their reactions appropriately: neither should they start with their line while the audience cannot hear it, as it could discourage the audience to laugh again, at least as much, the next time, nor should they wait until the house is completely silent again, because in that case it takes much (unnecessary) energy to get the momentum of the production up to speed again (Sievers, Stiver, Kahan, 1974: 191-2).

Not only words take a different emphasis and timing in comedy: much depends on the use of the body, particularly the face, for making the audience laugh at double-takes typical of boulevard comedy. Loriot in Germany, Rowan Atkinson in the United Kingdom and Jerry Lewis in the United States of America may serve as examples of actors well-known beyond the theatre to demonstrate how important an actor's face can be. If actors, who may be very good otherwise, lack that particular ability of facial control, audiences are likely to perceive them as comparatively less funny.

When it comes to casting, it is important and preferable not only to select actors who have a knack for boulevard comedy, but who are suitable to the character and the impact that character should have on the audience. In most plays in the repertory of boulevard comedy theatres, no character is dislikeable. Especially when the characters have to engage in erotic innuendo, much is left to the spectators' imagination. That imagination should have the potential of being pleasing, or at least neutral, but never unpleasant. The implications of this are straightforward in Flatow's *Verlängertes Wochenende*: when Ernst appears with just a towel around his waist, dripping wet, an actor with a slim appearance would make a better impression and would, therefore, be more suitable for the part than someone with a beer belly. It is a bit more complicated in Flatow's *Romeo mit grauen Schläfen*: when Frau Bethge, the housekeeper, is on the phone she describes how she tried to begin to seduce her previous employer(s). If the audience imagines her walking across the hall in a see-through nightgown, they should not feel uncomfortable with that imagination. On the other hand, if the director casts a very attractive woman in the part of Frau Bethge, the potential laugher at such a person expecting to impress a male employer would be diminished.

Directing Boulevard Comedy

As with any theatre production, part of the work of the director of boulevard comedy prior to the beginning of rehearsals consists in preparing the script. If the production in question is a world premiere, this may imply working with the dramatist, suggesting changes in the words, from the perspective not of the literary nature of the play, but its presentation in performance on stage with actors in front of an audience. Some lines that make much sense and are very witty when read on the page do not translate into the same effect on stage. The director is likely to bring the performance perspective to the text more strongly than the dramatist, especially if the writer is not also a director or actor. If directors work on the production of a play originally written in a language other than German, they may want to compare the translation provided by the publisher who holds the production rights and to whom royalties are due on behalf of the dramatist, with the original and make changes they see fit. Or they are inclined to make changes to the language without reference to the original on the basis of their own sense of the flow and efficiency of language and its impact on the audience.

To demonstrate the director's impact on the script, below is an excerpt from a scene in Samuel Taylor's *Gracious Living* (1978), translated as *Champagnerkomödie* by Jan Lustig. In the left column is the original German text, in the right column the revised version for the production of the Komödie Düsseldorf, in the spring of 1982, directed by Höckmann. The excerpt is from act 1, scene 3. Ageing former film star Donald Renshaw and his stage actress wife Victoria have been hired for a production of Shakespeare's *Hamlet* in London's West End: Donald is to play Polonius and Victoria Queen Gertrude. They are living at the Savoy Hotel, where the scene is set. Rehearsals are not really progressing as hoped—Donald is bored with the part and his American film star manners are not appropriate for the British cast and director. At the height of a row between Donald and Victoria, Daisy Bowhistle Tuttle suddenly appears in their room, unannounced.

Original German text	Alfons Höckmann's version
Daisy: Ich habe geklingelt und dann geklopft, aber ihr habt laut gesprochen, und dann ging das Telefon, stimmt's?	Daisy: Ich habe geklopft and geklopft, aber ihr habt laut gesprochen, und dann ging das Telefon, stimmt's?
Donald: Was wollen Sie?	Donald: Was wollen Sie hier?
Daisy: Ich habe vorher den Portier gebeten, heraufzurufen, ich wollte korrekt sein.	Daisy: Ich habe vorher den Portier gebeten, heraufzurufen, ich wollte korrekt sein.
Victoria: Also Sie waren es. Donald: Und ich habe ihm gesagt, daß er Sie wegschicken soll.	Victoria: Also Sie waren das? Donald: Ich hatte ihm doch gesagt, er soll Sie wegschicken
Daisy: Oh, das hat er auch gesagt. Er war sehr streng. Aber ich habe überall herumgeguckt und den Lift im hinteren Trakt gefunden.	Daisy: Ja, das hat er auch getan. Er war sehr streng. Aber ich habe ihn überlistet und jetzt bin ich hier.
(Sie hebt Donalds Schirm und Regenmantel vom Boden auf und legt sie ordentlich hin)	*(Sie hebt Donalds Schirm und Regenmantel vom Boden auf und legt sie ordentlich hin)*
Victoria: Sie hätten wirklich nicht kommen sollen, wir sind sehr beschäftigt.	Victoria: Sie hätten wirklich nicht kommen sollen. Sie sehen doch, daß wir beschäftigt sind.
Daisy: Ja, ich hab's gehört. Sie hatten einen prima Krach, nicht wahr? (…)	Daisy: Ja, das hab' ich gehört. Sie hatten einen prima Krach, nicht wahr? (…)
(Sie beginnt, die Kissen aufzuheben und auf Sofas und Sesseln zu verteilen)	*(Sie beginnt, die Kissen aufzuheben und auf Sofas und Sesseln zu verteilen)*
Donald: Lassen Sie das doch liegen.	Donald: Lassen Sie das doch liegen.
Victoria: Bitte machen Sie das nicht.	Victoria: Ja, lassen Sie alles liegen.

Daisy: Ich kann das doch nicht herumliegen lassen. Was würde das Zimmermädchen denken?	Daisy: Ich kann das doch nicht herumliegen lassen. Was würde das Zimmermädchen denken?
Donald: Ich habe gesagt, Sie sollen gehen.	Donald: Ich habe Sie doch gerade gebeten zu gehen. Haben Sie nicht gehört?

Apart from changing lines to make them more meaningful or more fluent for the actors to speak, references may need updating. A little further on in the scene from which the above excerpt was chosen, Daisy tells Donald and Victoria that thirty-five years ago, she had a relationship with Donald while she was working in the costume department. The film in question is rendered as *The Lives of a Bengal Lancer*. The title of the film suggests the kind of film this was, a blockbuster. In the 1982 Düsseldorf production, Paul Hubschmid played Renshaw. Hubschmid (1917-2002) was a famous German actor; he created the part of Henry Higgins in the first German production of *My Fair Lady*, playing altogether 2000 performances. One of his major successes in film, in 1958, was *Der Tiger von Eschnapur* (The Tiger of Eschnapur), directed by Fritz Lang, which is frequently repeated on German television and thus well known to the German audiences. Höckmann therefore replaced the unknown title *The Lives of a Bengal Lancer* with the one relating to the star of his production, Hubschmid, *Der Tiger von Eschnapur*. Daisy later refers to co-stars in other films Renshaw starred in, mentioning, in the original and its translation by Lustig, Ronald Colman and C. Aubrey Smith. No one in the audience at the Komödie Düsseldorf would have known those references and Höckmann replaced them with Vivien Leigh, Ronald Reagan (who was president of the United States in 1982) and Charles Laughton.

The director has to be aware of the conventions of boulevard comedy and must highlight them in production (Bloom, 1991: 98). Rehearsal time is not likely to allow the director either to teach comic technique or to explain to the cast which elements of the play carry potential for creating laughter. Directors of boulevard comedy theatre tend to agree that one of the most important skills they have to support in their actors is to ensure they play truthful characters in the first instance and not funny ones (Spier, 2003; Höckmann, 2001; Rummel, 2003; Helmer, 2003). In the first stages of the rehearsal process, the cast is likely to enjoy the comedy and laugh abundantly. However, a phase typically follows in which hardly anyone finds anything laughable any longer. In that phase it is particularly important for the director to make sure that the acting remains truthful and actors do not start trying too hard to be funny.

Rummel, Höckmann and others[1] fulfil the double function of actor and director in one person. They have developed what they describe as a paradoxical double-awareness of, as it were, observing themselves from the director's perspective while acting. Rummel, for instance, is able to develop his ideas of blocking and other aspects of the production while he studies the script closely in preparation for the rehearsals. Thus he can integrate himself into the process. In conversation, he agreed that it being an actor-director is a challenge for the other actors involved in the production and that special communication skills are needed to make the fellow-actors at ease with the actor-director as actor and at the same time also permit directorial intervention (2003).

At Düsseldorf's municipal theatre, Walter Adler, the director of a 1987 production of Shaffer's *Black Comedy* allegedly forbade his actors to laugh during rehearsals and the company was disappointed and surprised that their audiences did not laugh much either.[2] In recent productions of Labiche's farce *L'affaire Rue de Lourcine* (The Affair Rue de Lourcine), in Cologne (2001) and Düsseldorf (2003) the directors, Karin Beier and Fred Berndt faced typical boulevard comedy material: one morning, after a long night out, retired Lenglumé finds himself in bed with another man, Mistingue, whom he does not know—neither does he remember how this stranger ended up in his own bed. They are partially dressed and both are suffering from bad hangovers and loss of memory. They read in the newspaper that a girl was brutally killed the night before and the strange things they find in their pockets suggest to them that they were the murderers. Chaos ensues, particularly when it appears that Lenglumé's cousin saw them and knows what they did. In the end, the crises are resolved when Lenglumé realises that the newspaper in which they had read about the murder of the girl was in fact very old: on the night in question he and Mistingue could not possibly have murdered anyone. The cousin finally explains what really happened (he had only made vague comments so far, which Lenglumé and Mistingue had construed as further confirmation of their crime). Both Beier and Berndt sought to emphasise the darker elements of the play, how ordinary people can be trapped by one night's flawed behaviour; in their productions, the subject matter became an analysis of fear, an approach supported by the choice of Elfriede Jelinek, the 2004 literature Nobel laureate, to provide the German translation of the play.

Media Coverage

Based on her empirical research in the late 1970s, Leisentritt maintained that media reviews of boulevard comedy do not have much impact on potential spectators. Current artistic managers of boulevard comedy theatres tend to agree with this view.[3] Schlesselmann, for example, maintains that in Germany, bad reviews cannot ruin a show commercially by discouraging audiences to attend, as has been reported from the United States, at least with reference to New York's Broadway (Brustein, 1992). On the other hand, rave reviews do not necessarily guarantee a production's success either. The artistic managers of boulevard comedy theatres can excerpt good reviews for marketing purposes, sprinkled generously across flyers, souvenir brochures for individual productions or for announcements of the new season and in invitations to take out subscriptions. Since boulevard comedy theatres are private, typically not subsidised and rely on funding through box office receipts, advertising is more important for them than for municipal or state theatres. Thus boulevard comedy theatres are more dependent on public media acclaim than they like to admit. In addition, reviews are also important for the visiting artists, actors, designers and directors, whose livelihood depends on employment. Their employability is likely to rise when they keep getting good reviews and may equally be damaged by bad reviews. Although theatre managers will know from their own experience how fickle and unreliable the media can be and although they may weigh that against a bad review for a particular actor or director, a bad review may lead them to rethink their assessment of the artists they employ and may thus influence decisions when it comes to casting a future season. The same is true for good reviews. If they go along with an audience that clearly likes a performer praised by the media, artistic managers are more likely to re-employ such audience and media favourites.

Germany has several newspapers with national circulation, such as the dailies *Süddeutsche Zeitung*, *Frankfurter Allgemeine*, *Frankfurter Rundschau* and *Die Welt*, in addition to the weekly *Die Zeit*. They will normally not stoop to review boulevard comedy, regardless of where it is presented. Exceptions are what they would consider a special occasion, such as a leading director, or leading actors from the state or municipal theatre circuit giving their directorial or acting debuts at a boulevard comedy theatre. An example is the attention given to Ayckbourn's *Intimate Exchanges* in Berlin in *Die Welt* and *Frankfurter Allgemeine Zeitung* in 2001.

Audiences

The twenty-four boulevard comedy theatres in Germany together present an average of 161 performances per week, which adds up to around 8,000 per year. Any one week, some 80,000 spectators attend a boulevard comedy, or four million per year. This is a remarkable number of spectators for one genre and for private theatres. What kind of audiences does boulevard comedy attract? Leisentritt asked that question in her 1979 study. She found that most spectators come with friends or family to socialise and be entertained. There are more men than women in any one audience. The age group that is most strongly represented is 30-39, followed by 40-49. In comparison, in municipal and state theatres, those two age groups are least represented: here the age groups 60-69 and 20-29 are strongest. As far as occupations are concerned, salaried employees and homemakers are most strongly represented. Most spectators expect a happy ending, conventionally in form of a wedding. Based on those insights, Leisentritt's hypothesised that going to a boulevard comedy theatre fulfils primarily a need for security. Spectators do not seek to enrich their knowledge or self-knowledge; rather they seek to be reaffirmed and stabilised in the norms that constitute their lives. Leisentritt also concludes that boulevard comedy theatre has to be considered in the context not of theatre in general, but in the context of communication systems relevant to the leisure industry, such as television, cinema or even restaurants. She considers the existence and popularity of boulevard comedy theatres as an indication and symptom of a society whose individual members have, to a large extent, lost their abilities of communication. The safe world depicted on the boulevard comedy theatre stage, in line with the artificial level of socializing among the audience, cleverly manages to overshadow the fact that those spectators, representative of large sections of society, can say little, do not want to say much and have little to say anyway. Leisentritt regards any such critique of boulevard comedy theatre as a critique of the concept of sociability on which that genre of theatre is ultimately based; this in turn is a critique of society, which permits such a concept and such a reality of sociability to develop. Leisentritt develops a typology of boulevard comedies to support further her argument that plays in this genre of theatre are crafted in such a way as to fulfil the spectators' needs for happiness.

To summarise: acting in and directing boulevard comedy has its own specific rules that are distinct from acting in and directing comedy at other theatres, or acting in or directing plays in other genres of theatre. Productions at Germany's boulevard comedy theatres are usually not reviewed in the national media, with the exception of unusual casting, where stars from other genres of theatre, or from television and film, make forays into the boulevard comedy scene. Audiences tend to be broadly middle class, with the current dominant age range of late fifties and late sixties. Allegedly, they attend boulevard comedy theatre for the mere gratification of their sense of security, as the plays tend to confirm the status quo of life.

Notes

1 Wolfgang Spier, Claus Helmer, Herbert Herrmann, James von Berlepsch, Angelika Ober and René Heinersdorff.

2 Interview of the cast of *Komödie im Dunkeln*, Düsseldorfer Schauspielhaus, 1987.

3 As evidenced further by Martin Woelffer, Alfons Höckmann and Angelika Ober in interviews with the author.

CHAPTER FIVE

FUTURE RESEARCH POTENTIAL

Having discussed boulevard comedy theatre in Germany from the organizational and artistic perspectives, the way is prepared for further research into this phenomenon, such as: what are the criteria of good boulevard comedy in text and performance? What are the implications of the shift of generation among the boulevard comedy theatres' artistic managers and: what are the reasons for the continuing, even in creasing popularity of boulevard comedy in Germany? Brief comments on each of these issues will suffice.

Leisentritt's view of boulevard comedy theatre is clearly and inappropriately condescending. It is not appropriate to judge any boulevard comedy against what it never claims to be. It is neither a serious play nor a tragedy; it is not likely to (want to) lead its spectators to discover themselves, to deal with difficult intellectual issues, to question and query what they see and hear about. It wants to entertain; it wants to make its spectators laugh and no artist involved with boulevard comedy should feel inferior for it in comparison to other genres of theatre that have, historically, garnered more critical attention, understanding and acclaim. Similarly, media reviews of boulevard comedy should not judge this genre of theatre in terms appropriate for any other genre, but seek to apply criteria for quality from within the genre's boundaries, applying them both to text and performance. It is equally inappropriate to look down at audiences who choose to attend boulevard comedy productions because they seek entertainment, laughter, happiness and whatever other benefits they believe boulevard comedy to bring them.

Here are three possible criteria for quality: First, characters should be written and performed as rounded, realistic, plausible, life-like as possible and not merely, or even predominantly, as vehicles for comical lines or situation comedy. Secondly, actors should be cast to fit their characters: for example, a slim actor for Ernst in Flatow's *Verlängertes Wochenende* is more suitable for aesthetic reasons than one with a beer belly. The Komödie Dresden cast a 78-year-old former star, Evelyn Künneke (1921-2001) in the demanding part of Mrs. Chauvenet in Mary Chase's *Harvey*. What could have become a very successful production due to this particular casting decision turned out to be its downfall, both critically and commercially, because unfortunately the actress forgot most of her lines. Thirdly, a cast experienced in boulevard comedy theatre will have an advantage over a cast in which the majority of actors lack such experience. A production of Stefan Vögel's *Eine Gute Partie* may serve as an example. The play premiered at the Komödie im Marquardt, Stuttgart, in 2001 and was soon revived in almost all of the other boulevard comedy theatres across Germany. The production in Berlin and Hamburg was directed by and starred Wolfgang Spier. Actors experienced in boulevard theatre were also cast in the other roles. The new artistic manager of the Komödie Düsseldorf, Fuschl, directed two highly acclaimed, experienced actors as the leading couple, Alexander May and Christiane Hammacher. They were, however, relatively new to boulevard comedy. Approximately four months after its run in Düsseldorf, Fuschl's production was transferred to the *Komödie Frankfurt*. May maintained, in interview, that the long run of the production from Düsseldorf to Frankfurt had allowed the team to ease into their parts and thus improve the production (May, 2003). No doubt that is what happened; however, a production with a cast more experienced in boulevard comedy would not have started at the level the production was at in Düsseldorf soon after its opening night.

May played widower Fred Kowinski and when the curtain went up he was seen in a room that is very untidy. In the Spier production in Hamburg, the audience laughed when they saw the mess on stage as soon as the curtain opened. In Düsseldorf, the stage was littered with torn and crumpled kitchen roll, which, as the audience sees a little later, Kowinski uses to wipe his sweaty head repeatedly because it is so hot in his flat (it is summer during a heat wave). One of the important rules to note in writing, directing and acting in boulevard comedy is that no character should be dislikeable, because the audience's willingness to laugh depends on their liking the characters. The device of the kitchen roll brought May's character close to being disgusting and was thus potentially distancing and distracting to the audience, especially as the program notes stress that Kowinski is a grumpy but *likeable* old man. His son Leonhard comes and starts tidying up. In the Berlin/Hamburg production he tidies the room in such a way that he takes away all kinds of things from the floor and after he has finished, the place is at least halfway acceptable. In Düsseldorf/Frankfurt, he takes away most of the kitchen roll and some other things, but leaves some things where they are, sitting down on a chair instead of carrying on tidying up—the chair is placed on stage in such a way that anyone sitting on it is mostly hidden from the audience's view behind the table.

Fred's chess partner Walter is dressed leisurely, almost shabbily, for most of the production in Berlin/Hamburg, as one could expect from an elderly man who lives on his own. After his second major row with Fred he leaves, as does Rosalinda, the new housekeeper. When he comes back, it turns out that he now has Rosalinda as his own housekeeper and he is immaculately dressed, in suit and tie. This change comically mirrors Fred's own change in the way he was dressed before Rosalinda came into his life, in act 1, scene 1, in comparison with the beginning of act 1, scene 2, four weeks later. In the Düsseldorf/Frankfurt production Walter dresses immaculately right from the beginning of the play, allowing no change when he comes under Rosalinda's influence.

Once Rosalinda has left Fred, Leonhard hires a new housekeeper, a very young woman. In line with Fred's record with housekeepers, he manages to make her leave within one week. We see her when she is just leaving and Leonhard, who meets her in the staircase, is shocked because, as he comically puts it, she was a young woman when he hired her and now he could mistake her for her own grandmother, so much has she suffered under Fred's temper. In Berlin/Hamburg, the young woman, played by an actress in her early twenties, came across as very funny: it was hilarious that Fred could have reduced her to being totally dishevelled, run down, black rings under her eyes and crying uncontrollably. In Düsseldorf/Frankfurt, different young actresses played this part, but when they appeared in the same scene in the play, they were well made up, elegant, sexy, full of life and just bored and fed up with being patronised by the old man. This portrayal of the new housekeeper suggested that Leonhard was wildly exaggerating when he commented on her appearance and his earlier warnings against his father's record with housekeepers could only be exaggerated as well. Further research should be able to develop this argument and add criteria to the list.

As time progresses, more research will have to address the shift of generations among the artistic managers of Germany's boulevard comedy theatres. The long-established boulevard comedy theatres in Stuttgart, Berlin, München (Kleine Komödie am Max II) and Düsseldorf (Komödie Düsseldorf) have seen a change of their artistic management over the last six years and a similar change is likely to take place sooner or later in Bonn and Hannover. This change of artistic leadership amounts to a change of generation, because the artistic directors retiring at the age of sixty-five and upwards (Höckmann at the age of eighty) are making way for younger colleagues. The younger generation of artistic managers wants to change the kinds of plays they offer, the audiences they attract and the image that the public at large has of boulevard comedy. Having taken over existing theatres, they are aware of the need to keep the audiences that have been attending their theatres in some cases for decades. However, those audiences are also aging: the group that was most strongly represented among audiences in 1977, as studied by Leisentritt, was then aged thirty to thirty-nine; those patrons are now nearing their sixties. The second-strongest group was then aged forty to forty-nine; those patrons are now nearing their seventies. The younger artistic managers are aware of the need to recruit a new audience. It is possible to differentiate a number of trends in their decisions on what plays to put on, which in large part are based on what they believe is best for their recruitment efforts. First, they maintain a certain percentage of what they consider the traditional fare, some English and French authors, some Flatow: nothing too demanding intellectually. Second, they are keen to introduce plays to their repertory that are still broadly classified as comedy, but show darker undertones. Ayckbourn is a favourite in this context, but also comedies by Pierre Sauvil (*La surprise, La soleil pour deux*), Eric Emmanuel Schmitt (*Le Libertin*) and Stefan Vögel (*Eine Gute Partie, Süßer die Glocken* [Sweeter the bells, 2003], *Global Player* [2004], *Die süßesten Früchte* [The sweetest fruits, 2004]. The boulevard comedy theatres are able to cast well-known actors in the more serious plays who might not otherwise consider appearing in boulevard comedy; such new stars are likely to attract new audiences. While today's boulevard theatres in Paris have been successful with plays by Yasmina Reza, in Germany her plays have been taken up predominantly by state or municipal theatres. The third trend in the effort to recruit new audiences is to put on plays that intentionally play with nostalgia, attracting audiences to see a dramatization of something that has been meaningful in their lives, be it the life of an idol of their youth, or a sweeping memory of an era like the 1970s or the 1980s with all the music and issues relevant in those years.

It is interesting to compare the overall trends that characterise the repertory in long-established boulevard theatres that have recently undergone a generation change in their artistic management with relatively newly founded boulevard comedy theatres, such as Comödie Bochum, Comödie Duisburg, Comödie Wuppertal, Boulevard Münster and Komödie am Altstadtmarkt in Braunschweig, all of which came into existence with younger artistic managers. At these recently established theatres, there is not much of an attempt to do anything new: the seasonal repertories consist of traditional, well-established plays of the genre, with the usual one-off events. These theatres need to recruit their audiences from scratch, in competition with municipal theatres and may well have chosen predominantly established crowd-pleasers. The Theater an der Kö in Düsseldorf is different, in that it needed to make its name not only in competition with the municipal theatre, but also in competition with the Komödie Düsseldorf. For that reason, the artistic manager of the Theater an der Kö, René Heinersdorff, opted for a different repertory than the Komödie Düsseldorf, placing more emphasis on comedies with serious undertones, much like his peers who have taken over from retiring artistic managers of long established boulevard comedy theatres. Thus in the current range of boulevard comedy theatres in Germany, both tradition and innovation exist and are likely to remain.

Finally, further research may wish to address the question why there are twenty-four boulevard comedy theatres in Germany, growing in number and steadily successful at least as far as popularity and ticket sales are concerned? There are several related potential reasons:

- Boulevard comedies compensate for the often-bemoaned lack of humour in all areas of German society;
- Productions presented at municipal and state theatres do not appeal to the audiences who attend boulevard theatres—they may find them too pretentious, too didactic, too intent on the deep meaning of the plays, too avant-garde or too director-dominated.
- In the past twenty or thirty years, Germany has been considered a rich nation and the existence of boulevard comedy theatre is an indication of a well-to-do segment of society enjoying their affluence.
- At the time of this writing, Germany appears to be in a state of permanent financial crisis, with budgets in a number of federal states frozen and more and more voices of unease on the one hand and counter-views of the 'you don't know how lucky you are' kind on the other hand. In such a socio-political climate, boulevard comedy could be taking on the function of escapism.

Boulevard comedy theatre is a fascinating phenomenon of the German theatre scene. It is a rich object for research that has been long overdue.

Bibliography

Primary Sources

Flatow, C., *Der Mann, der sich nicht traut…*, Manuscript, Berlin, Felix Bloch Erben, 1973.
────── *Romeo mit grauen Schläfen*, Manuscript, Berlin, Felix Bloch Erben, 1985.
────── *Verlängertes Wochenende*, Manuscript, Berlin, Felix Bloch Erben, 1990.
────── *Zweite Geige,* Manuscript, Berlin, Felix Bloch Erben, 1991.
────── *Mein Vater, der Junggeselle,* Manuscript, Berlin, Felix Bloch Erben, 1994.
────── *Gesegnetes Alter*, Manuscript, Köln, Jussenhoven und Fischer, 1996.
Pillau, H., *Guten Tag, Herr Liebhaber*, Manuscript, Berlin, Felix Bloch Erben, 1997.

Secondary Sources

Anon., Der zerbrochene Traum, Katja Riemann kehrt am Kudamm ins Theater zurück, *Frankfurter Allgemeine Zeitung*, 05.03.2001.
Allen, P., *A pocket guide to Alan Ayckbourn's plays*, London, Faber, 2004.
Alisch, E., Interview with the author, tape recording, Düsseldorf, 28 October 2003.
Arvin, N. C., *Eugène Scribe and the French Theatre, 1815-1860,* New York, Benjamin Blom, 1924.
Bischoff, F., Interview with the author, tape recording, Kassel, 28 October 2003.
Bloom, M., *Thinking like a director*, London, Faber and Faber, 1991.
Bode, C., Interview with the author, 6 April 2003.
Bradby, D. and A. Sparks, *Mise end Scène, French Theatre Now*, London, Methuen Drama, 1998.
Brunet, B., *Le théâtre de boulevard*, Paris, Nathan, 2004.
Brustein R., 'An Embarrassment of Riches', *The New Republic online*, 16 March 1992, available at http://www.tnr.com/archive/brustein031692.html.

Chambers, C. (ed.) *The Continuum Companion to Twentieth Century Theatre*, London, Continuum, 2002.
Cooney, R., Program notes of the TiC, Wuppertal.
Corvin, M., *Le théâtre du boulevard*, Paris: Presses universitaires de France, 1989
Drechsler, U., *Die 'absurde' Farce bei Beckett, Pinter und Ionesco: Vor-und Überleben einer Gattung*, Tübingen, Gunter Narr, 1988.
Curth F., *Am Kurfürstendamm fing's an: Erinnerungen aus einem Gedächtnis mit Lücken*, München, Langen Müller, 2000.
Haida, P., *Komödie um 1900. Wandlungen des Gattungsschemas von Hauptmann bis Sternheim*, München, Fink, 1973.
Helmer, C., Interview with the author, tape recording, Frankfurt, 27 October 2003.
Hobson, H., *French Theatre Since 1830*, London, John Calder, 1978.
Höckmann, A., Interview with the author, tape recording, Düsseldorf, 9 April 2001.
Huxley, A., *Ape and Essence*, London, Chatto and Windus, 1951.
Isherwood, R. M., *Farce and Fantasy: Popular Entertainment in Eighteenth Century Paris*, New York, Oxford University Press, 1986.
Klotz, V., *Bürgerliches Lachtheatre: Komödie, Posse, Schwank, Operette*, Reinbek bei Hamburg, Rowohlt, 1987.
Komorr, R., Telephone conversation with the author, 14 March 2003.
Krause, T., 'Keine kann keifen wie Katja. Die Kudammbühnen arbeiten am Image, aber auch mit Katja Riemann finden sie nicht das Patentrezept' *Die Welt*, 05 March 2001.
Leisentritt, G., *Das eindimensionale Theater: Beitrag zur Soziologie des Boulevardtheatres*, München, Minverva, 1979.
Lynk, W. M. *Dinner Theatre: A Survey and Directory*, Westport, Connecticut, Greenwood, 1993.
Macroux, J. P., 'Georges Feydeau and the 'serious' farce', *Farce*, Themes in Drama, Volume 10, edited by James RedmondCambridge, Cambridge University Press, 1988, 131-143.
Maldeghem, C. P. von, 'Himmel, was werd' ich sagen', in Elert Bode (ed.), *Dem Vergnügen der Einwohner...: Das Alte Schauspielhaus und die Komödie im Marquardt in der Theaterstadt Stuttgart, 1976-2002*, Gerlingen, Bleicher, 2002, 147-49.
May, A., Interview with the author, tape recording, Frankfurt, 26 October 2003.
McCormick, J., *Melodrama Theatre of the French Boulevard*, Cambridge, Chadwyck Healey, 1982.

Meyer-Dinkgräfe, D. (ed.) *Who's Who in Contemporary World Theatre*, London, New York, Routledge, 2000.
Misiorny, S., Interview with the author, tape recording, Wuppertal, 21 July 2003.
Müller, T., Interview with the author, tape recording, Wuppertal, 21 July 2003.
Ober, A., Interview with the author, tape recording, Münster, 30 October 2003.
Prang, H., *Die Geschichte des Lustspiels. Von der Antike bis zur Gegenwart*, Stuttgart, Kröner, 1968.
Radler, R., *Knaurs Grosser Schauspielführer*, München, Droemersche Verlagsanstalt, 1985.
Root-Bernstein, M., *Boulevard Theater and Revolution in Eighteenth-Century Paris*, Ann Arbor, UMI Research P, 1984.
Rummel, D., Interview with the author, tape recording, Darmstadt, 19 July 2003.
Schlesselmann, G., Interview with the author, tape recording, Dresden, 4 April 2001.
Schoell, K., *Das französische Drama seit dem zweiten Weltkrieg, Bd. 1: Konventionelle Formen von Sartre bis Sagan*, Göttingen, Vandenhoeck und Ruprecht, 1970.
Shaw, G. B., 'How to Write a Popular Play' in his Preface to *Three Plays by Brieux*, New York, Brentano's, 1911.
Sievers, W. D., H.E. Stiver, Jr., S.Kahan, *Directing for the Theatre*, Dubuque, W.C.Brown, 1974.
Smith, L., *Modern British Farce. A Selective Study of British Farce from Pinero to the Present Day*, Totowa, Barnes and Noble, 1989.
Spier, W., Interview with the author, tape recording, Hamburg, 18 July 2003.
_____ *Dabei fällt mir ein... Lebensgeschichten*, Berlin, Henschel, 2004,
Stanton, S. and M. Banham (eds), *The Cambridge paperback Guide to Theatre*, Cambridge, Cambridge University Press, 1996.
Stürzebecher, R. F., Interview with the author, tape recording, Wuppertal, 20 July 2003.
Turk, H., 'Worüber lacht ihr? Genrekonventionen der Komödie im Spiegel der Übersetzung', in Paul, F., W. Ranke, B. Schultze, eds., *Europäische Komödie im übersetzerischen Transfer,* Tübingen, Narr, 1993.
Weckherlin, T., *Mit Boulevard gegen Dallas. Das Theater von Peter Zadek als kritisches Vergnügen*, Norderstedt, Books on Demand, 2001.

Wehinger, B., *Paris-Crinoline: Zur Faszination des Boulevardtheatres und der Mode im Kontext der Urbanität und der Modernität des Jahres 1857*, München, Wilhelm Fink, 1988.
Woelffer, M., Interview with the author, 3 April 2001.

APPENDIX A

CITIES WITH BOULEVARD COMEDY THEATRES

City	Name	Artistic director(s) 2004	Seating capacity	Range of ticket prices 2004 in €
Berlin	*Komödie*	Martin Woelffer	601	16-38
Berlin	*Theater am Kurfürstendamm*	Martin Woelffer	807	11-33
Bochum	*Comödie*	Patricia Frey, Rolf Berg and Jochen Schroeder	453	20-28
Bonn	*Contra Kreis Teater*	Katinka Hoffmann, Horst Johanning	261	14.50-25.50
Braunschweig	*Komödie am Altstadtmarkt*	Florian Battermann	321	17.10-24.10
Bremen	*Waldau-Theater Komödie*, from 1 October 2004 *Marth's im Waldau-Theater*	Michael Derda, from 1 October 2004 Susanne and Klaus Marth	505	18-30, from 1 October 2004 14-23

City	Name	Artistic director(s) 2004	Seating capacity	Range of ticket prices 2004 in €
Cologne	*Theater am Dom*	Inge Durek, Barbara Heinersdorff	376	15-27
Darmstadt	*TAP Komödie Darmstadt*	Dieter Rummel	156	15
Dresden	*Komödie Dresden*	Jürgen Wölffer, Jürgen Mai	643	12-37
Düsseldorf	*KomödieDüsseldorf*, from 2004 *Komödie Düsseldorf an der Steinstrasse*	Helmuth Fuschl, Paul Haizmann	376	13.50-32
Düsseldorf	*Theater an der Kö*	René Heinersdorff	400	14-27
Duisburg	*Comödie*	Patricia Frey, Rolf Berg and Jochen Schroeder	471	20-28
Frankfurt	*Komödie*	Claus Helmer	379	16.50-27
Hamburg	*Komödie Winterhuder Fährhaus*	Jürgen Wölffer, Michael Lang	554	9-31
Hannover	*Neues Theater*	James von Berlepsch	152	10-30
Karlsruhe	*Kammertheater Karlsruhe*	Heidi Vogel-Reinsch		10-16
Kassel	*Komödie Kassel*	Roland Heitz	145	8.50-17.50

City	Name	Artistic director(s) 2004	Seating capacity	Range of ticket prices 2004 in €
Münster	*Boulevard Münster*	Angelika Ober	121	18-26
Munich	*Komödie im Bayerischen Hof*	Margit Bönisch	574	21.90-36.30
Munich	*Kleine Komödie am Max II*	Ralf Komorr und Fritz Hendel	577	15-34
Nürnberg – Fürth	*Comödie im Berolzheimerianum*	Volker Heißmann and Martin Rassau	90	13-28
Stuttgart	*Komödie im Marquardt*	Carl Philip von Maldeghem	378	7.50 – 17.50
Wuppertal	*TiC Theater in Cronenberg*	Ronald F. Stürzebecher	80	8-16
Wuppertal	*m&m theatre*	Sabine Misiorny and Tom Muller	80	8-16
Wuppertal	*Comödie Wuppertal*	Patricia Frey, Rolf Berg and Jochen Schroeder	195	20-28

Appendix B

Plays

Author	Original Play Title	English Title	German Title	Year
Ayckbourn, Alan	*Season's Greetings*		*Schöne Bescherungen*	1980
Ayckbourn, Alan	*Time of my Life*		*Glückliche Zeiten*	1992
Ayckbourn, Alan	*Intimate exchanges*		*Raucher/Nichtraucher*	1982
Ayckbourn, Alan	*Henceforward*		*Ab Jetzt*	1997
Barillet, Pierre and Jean-Pierre Grédy	*Fleur de Cactus*	*Cactus flower*	*Die Kaktusblüte*	1963
Battermann, Florian	*Weekend mit Winnetou*	*Weekend with Winnetou*		1998
Battermann, Florian	*Drei plus eins gleich Halleluja*	*Three plus one equals Halleluja*		2000
Battermann, Florian	*Drum prüfe ewig, wer sich bindet*	*Therefore, check each other out forever…*		2002
Black, Penny	*Making Babies*		*Making Babies*	2003
Camoletti, Marc	*Boeing-Boeing*	*Boeing-Boeing*	*Boeing-Boeing*	1961
Chapman, John	*Dry Rot*		*Dry Rot*	1954

Author	Original Play Title	English Title	German Title	Year
Chapman, John and Ray Cooney	*Not now, darling*		*Jetzt nicht, Liebling*	1967
Chapman, John and Ray Cooney	*There goes the bride*		*Und das am Hochzeitsmorgen*	1974
Chapman, John and Ray Cooney	*Move over Mrs. Markham*			1969
Chapman, John and Ray Cooney	*My Giddy Aunt*			1967
Chatten, Claus	*Klassentreffen*	*Class reunion*		2003
Conti, Fernando	*Wann wird's mal wieder richtig Sommer*	*When are we going to have a proper summer again?*		2003
Cooney, Ray	*Run for your Wife*		*Taxi, Taxi*	1982
Cooney, Ray	*Caught in the Net: Run for your Wife, Again*		*Lügen haben Junge Beine*	2001
Flatow, Curth	*Verlängertes Wochenende*	*Extended Weekend*		1990
Flatow, Curth	*Der Mann, der sich nicht traut…*	*Happy Wedding*		1973
Flatow, Curth	*Ein gesegnetes Alter*	*Blessed Age*		1996

Author	Original Play Title	English Title	German Title	Year
Flatow, Curth	*Romeo mit grauen Schläfen*	*Romeo with grey temples*		1985
Flatow, Curth	*Zweite Geige*	*Second Violin*		1991
Flatow, Curth	*Mein Vater, der Junggeselle*	*My father the bachelor*		1994
Flatow, Curth	*Vater einer Tochter*	*Father of a daughter*		1966
Goetz, Curth	*Ingeborg*	*Ingeborg*		1922
Goetz, Curth	*Hokuspokus*	*Hokuspokus*		1953
Hadeke, Sabine	*der himmel ist weiss*	*the sky is white*		2003
Labiche, Eugène	*L'affaire rue du Lourcine*	*The Affair in the rue du Lourcine*	*Die Affäre in der rue du Lourcine*	1857
LaBute, Neil	*The shape of things*		*Das Maß der Dinge*	2003
Lausund, Ingrid	*Hysterikon*	*Hysterikon*	*Hysterikon*	2003
Levrey, Patricia	*A cloche pied*	*Break a leg*	*Herz-und Beinbruch*	1998
Magnier, Claude	*Oscar*	*Oscar*	*Oscar*	1958
Magnier, Claude	*Monsieur Masure*	*A Clear-Cut Case*	*Ein Klarer Fall*	1954
Pillau, Horst	*Guten Tag, Herr Liebhaber*	*Good day, Mr. Lover*		1997
Pillau, Horst	*Buddha spricht nur mit Männern*	*Buddha talks to men only*		

Author	Original Play Title	English Title	German Title	Year
Pillau, Horst	Mein Vater, der Wessi	My father from West Germany		2001
Pillau, Horst	Nur noch Ausatmen	Only exhale		1990
Phillip, Gunter	Da wird Daddy staunen	Daddy will be surprised		2000
Price, Stanley	The Starving Rich		Joghurt für Zwei	1973
Sauvil, Pierre	Soleil pour deux	Sun for Two	Sonne für Zwei	1998
	La Surprise	The Surprise	Die Überraschung	1999
Schmitt, Eric Emmanuel	Le Libertin	The Free Spirit	Der Freigeist	1997
Scribe, Eugène	Un verre d'eau	A Glass of Water	Das Glas Wasser	1840
Shaffer, Peter	Black Comedy		Komödie im Dunkeln	1965
Simon, Neil	The Last of the Red Hot Lovers		Der letzte der feurigen Liebhaber	1969
Taylor, Samuel	Gracious living		Champagnerkomödie	1978
Thomas, Brandon	Charley's Aunt		Charleys Tante	1892
Vögel, Stefan	Süßer die Glocken	Sweeter the Bells		2003
Vögel, Stefan	Ein Gute Partie	Check, Mate		2002
Wittenbrink, Frank	Sekretärinnen	Secretaries		2000

INDEX

Achard, Marcel 9, 36
Adler, Walter 86
Albaum, Lars 36 – 8
Alexey, Alexander 38
Alisch, Ernst 80
Allen, Paul 35
Anouilh, Jean 9, 21
Antoine, André 9
Aristophanes 9
Arvin, N.C. 8
Atkinson, Rowan 82
Au, Michael von 31
Ayckbourn, Alan 29, 31-3, 35-6, 40, 63, 73-5, 87, 93

Baer, Richard 37, 37
Barillet, Pierre 9, 36, 39, 40, 50
Barlach, Ernst 21
Barlow, Patrick 38
Battermann, Florian 19, 26, 27, 37, 38, 62
Becker, Gert 39
Beier, Karin 86
Benfield, Derek 36, 38
Berg, Rolf 19, 29
Berlepsch, James von 18, 26, 28, 62, 89
Berlin 1, 12, 13, 18, 23, 28, 30-2, 34, 73, 76, 79, 87, 91, 92
Bernard, Tristan 9
Berndt, Fred 86
Beth, Gunther 36-8
Bischoff, Frank 79
Black, Penny 33
Bloom, M. 85

Bobrick, Sam 36
Bochum 1, 19, 20, 29, 34, 93
Bode, Christa 32, 74
Bode, Elert 32, 39. 40
Bodinus, Jens 37
Böhling, Dirk 36, 38
Bönisch, Margret 19, 33
Bogdanov, Michael 24
Bohnet, Folker 36, 38
Bonn 1, 18, 37, 92
Braband, Folke 37
Bradby, David 11
Brandauer, Klaus Maria 31
Braunschweig 1, 19, 26, 37, 93
Braut, Frigga 19, 20
Braut, Ingrid 12, 16, 17, 18, 19, 20, 21, 22, 30, 33
Bremen 2, 19, 28, 34
Breth, Andrea 74
Brook, Peter 24
Brooks, Hindi 36-7
Bruckner, Ferdinand 13
Brustein, Robert 87
Brunet, B. 4
Busse, Jochen 37, 38

Camoletti, Marc 36, 37, 52
Capell, Barbara 36-8
Chambers, Colin 3
Chapman, John 36, 39, 63
Chase, Mary 36, 90
Chatten, Claus 37, 76
Chodorov, Jerome 36
Churchill, Donald 36
Colman, Ronald 85

Cologne 1, 18, 22, 23, 37
Conti, Ferdinando 37
Cooney, Ray 3, 36-8, 63, 69, 73
Copeau, Jacques 9
Corvin, M. 3
Coward, Noel 20, 36

Dagover, Lil 22
Darmstadt 1, 23, 27, 34, 37, 79
Derda, Michael 19
Deval, Jacques 9, 36
Dorin, Françoise 9, 36
Dresden 1, 13, 18, 19, 23, 28, 29, 31-4, 90
Duisburg 1, 93
Dunham, Tony 38
Durek, Inge 18
Düsseldorf 1, 12, 15, 16, 17, 18, 19, 21, 22, 23, 29, 30, 33, 34, 83, 91, 93, 94
Dumas, Alexandre 8

Exner, Markus 79

Faulkner, William 21
Fehn, Gerhard 24
Feydeau, Georges 9, 10, 36, 63
Flatow, Curth 10, 36-9, 40-73, 77, 82
Frankfurt 1, 18, 29, 30, 79, 91, 92
Frankh, Pierre 38
Frey, Patricia 29
Frisby, Terence 36
Fürth 1, 34, 76
Fuschl, Helmuth 12, 16, 19, 30, 91

Géraldy, Paul 9, 36
Gershe, Leonard 36
Giehse, Therese 21

Goethe, Johann Wolfgang 20
Goetz, Curth 13, 20, 29, 36, 38, 40
Goldoni, Carlo 5, 13
Goodheart, William 36
Görtz, Franz Josef 26
Grédy, Jean-Pierre 9, 36, 39, 40, 50
Greiffenhagen, Gottfried 76
Grillparzer, Franz 20, 21

Habeke, Sabine 33
Haizmann, Paul 12, 16, 19, 30
Hamburg 1, 3, 13, 18, 19, 23, 28, 31, 34, 91, 92
Hammacher, Christiane 91
Hannover 1, 18, 26, 34, 38. 92
Hatheyer, Heidemarie 21
Hauptmann, Gerhart 20
Heilbronn 1, 2, 32
Heinersdorff, René 18, 23, 29, 31, 36, 37, 38, 89
Heinze, Horst 22
Heinze, Annemarie 22
Heitz, Roland 19, 24, 25, 38
Helmer, Claus 18, 30, 79, 80, 85, 89
Hendel, Fritz 31
Hepburn, Audrey 40
Herrmann, Herbert 32, 37, 89
Hinz, Werner 21
Hobson, Harold 10
Höckmann, Alfons 12, 16-19, 21, 22, 30, 33, 80, 81, 83-86, 89, 92
Hörner, Frank 37
Hoffmann, Katinka 18
Home, William Douglas 36
Hubschmid, Paul 85
Huxley, Aldous 9

Isherwood, Robert, 10
Isitt, Debbie 36, 39

Jacobs, Dietmar 36-8
Jacoby, Wilhelm 39
Jamin, Peter H. 38
Jelinek, Elfriede 86
Johanning, Horst 18

Kahan, S. 82
Kalmbach, Natascha 39
Karasek, Daniel 31
Karlsruhe 1, 19, 34
Kassel 1, 19, 24, 30, 34, 38, 76, 79
Kaufmann, Andreas 39
Kaufmann, Oskar 13
Klotz, Volker 10
Kesselring, Joseph 30
Knuth, Gustav 21
Komorr, Ralph 31, 32
Krasna, Norman 36
Krause, Tilmann 74
Künneke, Evelyn 90

Labiche, Eugène 8, 9, 36, 63, 86
LaButa, Neil 33
Landgrebe, Gudrun 32
Lang, Fritz 85
Lang, Michael 19
Langner, Manfred 37
Lateika, Horst 24
Laufenberg, Eric Uwe 74, 75
Laufs, Carl 39
Laughton, Charles 85
Laurence, Charles 37
Lausund, Ingrid 33
Leidesdorff, Ernst 19
Leigh, Vivien 85
Leipnitz, Harald 23

Leisentritt, Gudrun 3, 87, 88, 93
Lessing, Gotthold E 30
Levin, Ira 38
Levrey, Patricia 51
Lewis, Jerry 82
Lindtberg, Leopold 21
Loriot 36, 39, 40, 75, 82
Ludwig, Ken 36
Lustig, Jan 83, 85
Lynk, D.C. 4

Macroux, Paul 10
Magnier, Claude 29, 39
Mai, Gisela 31
Mai, Jürgen 19
Maldeghem, Carl Philip von 19, 24, 30
Marceau, Felicien 9, 36
Mares, Rolf 19
Marth, Klaus 34
Marth, Sabine 34
Matthau, Walter 40
May, Alexander 80, 91
McCormick, J. 4
Mertens, Michael 31
Misiorny, Sabine 2, 27, 30
Moissi, Johanna 21
Molière 29
Morgenrot, Daniel 31
Mortiers, Gerard 24
Mozart, Wolfgang Amadeus 21
Müller, Tom 2, 27, 30
Münster 1, 12, 13, 14, 15, 17, 19, 25, 26, 32, 34, 39, 79, 93
Munich 1, 18, 19, 23, 29, 31, 33, 34, 38, 92

Nagel, Ivan 24
Naughton, Bill 24

Neubert, Gerd 37

Ober, Angelika 13, 14, 25, 26,
  32, 39, 79, 89,
Ober, Elke 26, 39
Oehme, Peter 21
Oesterrieth, Marie 37
O'Neill, Eugene 21

Pertwee, Michael 36
Peymann, Claus 24
Philipp, Gunter 16, 51
Pillau, Horst 36, 39, 51, 55, 62, 71
Pinkus, Frank 36, 39
Pittermann, Peter 26, 39
Plautus 9
Pörtner, Paul 39
Prang, H. 2
Price, Stanley 51

Quadflieg, Christian 29
Quadflieg, Will 21

Raeck, Kurt 13
Reagan, Ronald 85
Redmond, James 10
Reinhardt, Max 13
Reza, Yasmin 9, 11, 36, 93
Riemann, Katja 31, 74, 75
Rix, Brian 3
Roman, Laurence 38, 39
Root-Bernstein, M. 5, 6
Roussin, André 9, 36
Rummel, Dieter 21, 23, 27, 28, 79, 80, 85, 86
Rummel, Monika 27

Sagan, Françoise 9, 36
Sandrock, Adele 13

Sardou, Victorien 8, 9, 36
Sartre, Jean Paul 9, 21
Sauvil, Pierre 36, 38, 55, 93
Schaufuß, Hans-Hermann 19, 20
Schiller, Friedrich 20, 21
Schlesselmann, Gerd 18, 23, 24, 29, 33, 87
Schmitt, Erich Emanuel 9, 11, 36, 55, 93
Schmitt, Saladin 20
Schoell, K. 2
Schröder, Jochen 19, 29
Scribe, Eugène 8, 9
Seibel, Volker 28
Shaffer, Peter 36
Shakespeare, William 9, 21
Shaw, George Bernard 8
Sieger, Dieter 13, 14
Sievers, W.D. 82
Simon, Neil 4, 35, 36, 37, 40
Slade, Bernard 36
Sparks, Annie 11
Spier, Wolfgang 32, 37, 80, 81, 85, 89
Stein, Peter 24
Stiver, H.E. 82
Stroux, Karl Heinz 22
Stürzebecher, Ronald 19, 25, 28
Stuttgart 1, 2, 19, 24, 29, 30, 32, 34, 39, 91, 92

Taylor, Samuel 46, 51, 83
Thiesler, Sabine 36
Thomas, Brandon 20, 36
Thomas, Peter 22
Thomas, Robert 39
Thompson, T.B. 27
Travers, Ben 3, 63
Turk, Horst 68

Uhry, Alfred 38

Veber, François 36, 37
Vögel, Stefan 36, 37, 39, 54, 71, 91, 93
Vogel-Reinsch, Heidi 19

Wälterlin, Oskar 21
Walls, Tom 3
Watkyn, Arthur 36
Weckherlin, T. 8
Wilde, Oscar 21

Williams, Simon 36
Wittenbrink, Frank 33, 76
Wölffer, Christian 13
Wölffer, Hans 13
Wölffer, Jürgen 13, 18, 37
Woelffer, Martin 13, 23, 31, 37, 73, 74, 76, 79, 89
Wouk, Herman 21
Wuppertal 1, 18, 19, 25, 27, 30, 34, 39, 93

Yeldham, Peter 36, 37